Sieste in Peace

An artful pageturner of a cozy mystery

Christa Bakker

Counting Blessings

Contents

1

I want to see your pants

'Lift your skirt higher! I want to see your pants.' The things you say when you're a peekaboo pin-up photographer...

As a special favour to my friend Marie Madora, I was making an attempt at herding cats. Group shoots had never been my favourite and I usually tried to avoid them. My slightly naughty style of picture always made my subjects giddy, but in a group they tended to veer towards rowdy. And then, of course, there was always that one who had been taken hostage and wasn't particularly comfortable. Today it was a timid woman named Amélie, plucking at her false eyelashes while the others preened in the dressing room mirror.

But I'd deal with her later. Right now, Marie had her moment in the spotlight – she practically danced towards the heap of magazines strewn about as though she'd tripped on them, then sat daintily on top. I'd met her a few months after I'd moved back to Saint-Maurice and had done a shoot with her before, but she'd made a mess of the pictures. Although she'd been born with a left arm that didn't extend beyond her elbow, that hadn't been what held her back. Today, holding up her skirt and petticoat with her hand and putting her stump to her surprised mouth, she'd finally got the hang of my style. And now that she didn't hide her face under layers of make-up any more, she'd found confidence in her natural beauty. So much, in fact, that she'd convinced me to do a group shoot with her and her friends. Paid, this time, since I wasn't trying to find out if she'd murdered anyone.

Looking back, it seemed outrageous that I'd ever suspected her, but then, I'd learned in the meantime that killers aren't always the ones you'd suspect. Just as the people who become your friends aren't always the ones you'd think. Like this bunch of women right here, who seemed mismatched in every way but were clearly very close friends. My friend Marie was a Dutch woman who'd made a fortune in inflatables. She'd brought a short, perky, black-haired Irish woman named Moira who said she liked things quiet and traditional, but who was staying in the new Centre de Prédiction a few hills over in Blacenas. Combining health and wellness with a kind of divination, that place was anything but traditional, though in spite of local and national advertising, I still didn't know exactly what it was or did.

One of Marie's other friends, Nienke, was also Dutch. I knew her because she was married to my mother's friend Cédric. Her fiery red hair streaked with a blondish grey was a contrast to her gentle character. She spent most of her days crafting and knitting brightly coloured scarves and socks for orphans in Eastern Europe.

The only woman in the group who made me nervous was Amélie. While the others were now laughing and pointing at the photos on the wall, she couldn't get into the spirit of my art style. In my experience, women like her were only thinking over and over again how much they did not want to be here, instead of opening their minds to the possibility of having a good time. I had some tricks up my sleeve, of course, but they required time alone with the woman in question, which often made the rest of the group feel abandoned.

And that is why I employed an assistant. He could take care of the group while I took one of them aside, and by the time I would have converted the one, the others would hardly have noticed I was gone. That was the plan. Usually. Today, my assistant hadn't bothered to show up yet. Had he not knocked on my door asking to be my assistant? Should he not then at least try to be here when I needed him?

Ordinarily, I would have managed and later rubbed his face in the fact that I didn't need any men in my business, least of all him, but Thibault had not been himself lately. So not only was he not here to help me, he added to my troubles by making me worry about him.

I finished up with Marie and had to make a decision on whether I'd take Amélie aside to do her solo shoot first or take everyone outside for the group photos. I wanted to capture the group while their energy was still high. But if Amélie wasn't comfortable, she'd ruin the group photos too.

I could, of course, try calling her by some animal name, like Beau always did, but I didn't think that particular trick would work to my advantage. Wrong gender. Also wrong face, wrong age, and wrong character to call a woman my goat or my shrimp. Most women would let a handsome young man get away with flirty name-calling, but Julie Belmain, thirty-one and counting, was too dignified to make that technique work, despite her not-so-dignified profession. Ask all my thoroughly dignified ancestors: a Belmain sets the right example. They were turning in their graves because of me already, so I'd better not add insult to injury.

Maybe I could use the big fan? The skirt would go up, but the success of the picture depended on the client's reaction. A surprised smile was what I was going for, not the embarrassed blush and deer-in-the-headlights eyes I would probably get. I suppressed a sigh and straightened my back, determined not to show my apprehension as I joined the group to fetch Ms Difficult.

Without my camera present, even she was having a giggle. With their colourful fifties-style dresses, red lips, and hairsprayed pin curls, the group looked transported from the Golden Age of Hollywood.

'But don't you agree?' Marie was saying. 'It's weird being the same age as old people.' The others protested with fervour, and she hastily added, 'Present company excluded, naturally.'

Amélie grinned. 'And then suddenly your spouse is getting old. It's bad enough that *I'm* sagging, but why are the outsides of his beautiful legs suddenly bald? I did not sign up for this!'

Moira, the dark-haired woman, who had a prominent cleft lip scar, snorted. 'Yeah, your life sucks.'

'What? You know my son. He's so annoying, France should use him as their secret weapon in the next war.'

A clamour of both objections and concurrences erupted, and I raised my camera and my voice to get them back to the matter at hand. Group shoot it was. Maybe the other women would sweep Amélie up in their excitement.

'Ladies! I'd like you all to line up on the edge of the pool, please.'

While the others whooped and cheered, Amélie's smile withered as she trudged after her friends. This could only end in disaster, but what could I do? I racked my brain for something – anything – to spark some enthusiasm without putting her negative attitude in the spotlight.

'Amélie, you go in the middle. I'm going to make you the centre of attention. Come on girls, group hug around Amélie.

Show her some love!' It worked, if only a little. At least Amélie relaxed and even showed a little smile, but she was far from excited. 'All right, now when I say so, raise your skirts as if you're being splashed. Unfortunately, my assistant is not—'

'Willing to get wet. But I can splash with the best of them.' Beau sauntered out into the garden, carrying a fishing rod. Though tardy to the point of we'll-talk-about-this-later, his timing was perfect. I didn't know whether to be angry or relieved, but I couldn't give voice to either in front of my clients, so he was forgiven. For now.

'Don't think you'll catch much here.'

It sounded like a joke to the women, but Beau knew me well enough to hear the reprimand. There were only nine years between us, but that didn't make me want to mother him any less. Instead of giving an explanation though, he turned with flawless aim to Amélie and bestowed upon her his starlight smile. 'You look amazing.'

Magic. There was no other way to explain it. How else could he know exactly who needed the boost, and how else could he deliver that boost so accurately? Amélie seemed to grow two inches, her chest rising, and her eyes starting to sparkle. She pushed the others into position, lifted her skirt, and took on the perfect surprised pose, while Beau found a thick branch at the bottom of the garden to hit the water with.

The challenge here was to get all four women to look good at the same time. Hopefully while the water droplets were still flying, but that's what post-production is for. I switched my camera to burst mode and signalled Beau that I was ready. He knelt by the pool while I told the ladies to move their chins forward and down. They dutifully obeyed me, but forgot immediately when Beau hit the water with the stick and they all got soaked. My camera rapidly fired off the shots. If I could have, I would have crossed my fingers, superstitious as it was. With a shot like this, you need a lot of luck.

While the women howled with laughter and tried to chide Beau, I quickly withdrew into the shade to check the pictures. One good one. Two. Maybe three. That would do. I let out a breath. After my failed attempt with Amélie, my confidence had been dented, but this helped me get back on top.

'That was beautiful, *mes dames*. Can I ask you to retire to the dressing room for your next outfits and a refresh of your make-up?'

As they filed back into the studio, giggling and shaking water off their hands, I shot off a text to my make-up artist Maile to fix Amélie first so I could take her solo shots while the others were still changing.

'Caught anything?' My tone was light, but I had my scolding-mother face on.

Beau avoided my eyes. 'Oh, I don't use a hook. I just tie a piece of bread to the line and watch the fish nibble on it.'

'How humane. It must have been fascinating to watch.'

'Not as much as the change in that woman's face just now.'

Oh! Could he get any more obnoxious? He knew I'd needed him just now, and he thought that made up for his lack of work ethic. Well, we'd see about that!

After the shoot, of course. I still needed him.

I threw him one last seething look, which he pointedly ignored, and joined the women in the dressing room.

Amélie was enjoying herself now that I didn't want anything from her. 'They call this olive skin, though I have yet to encounter an olive of this colour. They're either black, green, or purple, so someone with real olive skin would have to be from outer space.' She held up her arm in demonstration.

Moira sighed. 'I wouldn't mind olive skin. Mine's the colour of an old newspaper.' She looked wistfully at the back of her hands.

'There are skin-coloured olives,' Nienke remarked. 'But they're called blonde olives, though anyone with hair that colour would not be called a blonde. Red, maybe, but most of them still have a tinge of green on them. It's not a healthy colour, for skin or hair,' she decided.

'Wait till you see those mealworms at the Centre de Prédiction,' Moira said. 'Most of them look green, whether it's from starvation, envy, old age, or some natural beauty mask.'

Marie rolled her eyes. 'Why do you go there if all you do is rant about the people and the things they do? It's not like it's a cheap place. You're still welcome to stay with me, you know.'

Moira shook her head with a grin. 'No! I love ranting! I'm the only one who pays through the nose to *not* partake in the sage burning, mud baths, and floatation therapy. My wellness goes up leaps and bounds watching other people do that to themselves while I gorge on a smuggled-in bag of crisps.'

The others chuckled, though I heard Nienke mutter, 'I burn sage sometimes. It's very soothing. Though a little masculine.'

My make-up artist signalled me as she swivelled Amélie's chair, and I took a step forward. 'Ladies, I'm sorry to break up your fun, but it's time for Amélie's shoot. As you were.'

I took Amélie, who had completely defrosted, through to my office, where I'd laid out a few poses she could choose from. The others had already done so on their first appointment, but Amélie had been hesitant and I'd told her she could always choose in the moment. Now, she stepped up to my desk and immediately pointed to Hold the Phone.

'If I do that one, could you make my legs look slimmer at the top?'

I smiled apologetically. 'I don't shave off pounds, but I do make peaches of oranges when it comes to skin.'

She thought about that, then nodded. A small smile slowly grew into a bigger one. '*Oui*... Yes, that would work. Let's do it.'

The rest of the session went like a dream. With Amélie now excited, it seemed all my pictures were winners. I'd have trouble weeding later on. As much as I hated to admit it, I'd come to rely on Thibault for situations like these. Somehow, he could solve a problematic attitude in two seconds flat. After his late entry, he'd initially been his charming self, smiling and joking around, making all the women blush in turn by calling them his tigress or his lamb. But as the shoot progressed, he got more and more reserved, until Céline, the baker's daughter, honked to signal the arrival of my end-of-shoot cupcakes, and Beau disappeared altogether.

'Something wrong?' Marie asked while the others attacked the cupcakes.

I shrugged. 'He's been like that since the start of the year. But you know, he's twenty-two. Maybe being a photographer's assistant isn't his dream job after all.'

Her mouth fell open. 'He's leaving?'

'I don't know.' I stared at the cast-iron spiral staircase leading to his apartment above the studio. 'He hasn't said anything, but it's always a possibility.'

After successfully repressing the thought for the past few weeks, finally verbalising it made me sad. Beau had only been with me for a little over six months, and most of that time I'd spent thinking of ways to get rid of him. But now that he himself might be thinking of leaving, I realised I'd grown attached to having him here.

Marie gave me a pitying look. 'Bigger dreams for his future, *hein*?'

'I suppose I have those too. For him, I mean. He's been learning about photography, and you should see his drawings! He's going places.' I sighed. 'I just hoped he'd take a little longer getting there.'

Marie squeezed my hand, then reached for a cupcake and held it out to me. 'Thibault replacement therapy?'

I burst out in a surprised laugh. 'You're terrible! I'd get fat within a week.'

'Oh, just this once.' She waved away my objection with her stump. 'We're going on a hike right after this, so you need the energy.'

I huffed. 'Only because this is a cherry-filled one. Fruit is healthy, *non*?'

'Exactly.'

We both grinned as we took a mouthful of butter and sugar.

Nienke had already finished her cupcake and was talking to Céline, who was lingering after her delivery to share a cupcake with the group. 'So, how is the boyfriend?' She stretched the word until it made Céline blush. 'Going on, what, four months now?'

Céline nodded with a smile. 'Yes, he's... nice.'

All the older women, including me, huffed and puffed and threw our hands in the air.

'Nice! That's no word to describe your boyfriend. We've seen him. We know he's "nice".' Marie made giant air quotes to underline her point. 'Come on, you have to give us more than that. Is he romantic? Does he take you out to dinner?' She turned and added to Amélie, 'You know, Maarten always let me pay my share when we were dating. Dutch men, puh!'

'Yes, I remember,' Amélie said, her eyebrows flying together in shocked indignation, even after all this time.

'Does he give you presents?' Moira continued the interrogation. 'Is he a good kisser?'

Everyone stared at her.

'You don't even know him,' Nienke said.

'Well, I'm still curious.' Moira shrugged but changed the topic. 'I should go. There's an adult wrapping session at two that I have to go laugh at.'

'Adult... wrapping?' Amélie made a face as if she were contemplating the existence of the liger.

'Yup.' Moira's eyes shone with glee. 'You put your knees to your chest and then you're swaddled like a baby and gently rocked back and forth. I've seen grown men start to cry! Not sure if that was because the therapy was working or because the wrap was too tight, but it was beautiful. Don't want to miss that.'

I blinked several times before I could process the mental image she'd created, and it took a few seconds for anyone else to say anything.

'I should go too,' Marie announced, getting up from the white leather couch. 'Girls, thank you all for a wonderful morning. It has been amazing!' She turned to me, pointing a finger. 'I'll be back in half an hour – make sure you are ready to go.'

They all hugged and tumbled out the door, high on fun and sugar. I waved them off with a smile but then turned back and sighed, dreading what was coming next. Ordinarily, my sessions lasted from ten till twelve, but we'd scheduled Marie and friends earlier so she and I could go on a hike before lunch. The hike had been in our diaries for ages because I knew I'd need distraction on this day, but I hadn't counted on Beau choosing this moment to stage a mutiny.

I dragged myself up the steps and knocked on his door. 'Thibault?'

The springs in my great-aunt's old sofa creaked and the door lock clicked. Beau let the door fling open, already retreating back to his seat and picking up his sketchbook. I closed the door behind me and sat in one of the two old armchairs.

'So?' I tried, not really sure where to begin.

'So, what?'

'Can you put down your drawing and talk to me?'

He sighed like a sulky teenager and dramatically threw his pad on the couch next to him.

Thinking he might start talking if I was just there for him, I folded my hands in my lap and waited, but all he said was, 'What?'

'You know what.' It came out more frustrated than I'd intended and I adjusted my tone to a more talk-inducing one. 'You've not been the most sociable of people lately, but you've never shown up late for work before. As an employer, that doesn't make me happy, but as a friend, I'd like to help if I can. What's going on?'

'You never start before ten.'

'I reminded you yesterday, and you said it was fine. Where were you?'

'Drawing.'

As usual. But in case that was his chosen career path, I wanted him to know I supported that. 'Can I see?'

'No.' He reached to his pad and turned it over.

Biting my tongue so I wouldn't comment on his childish behaviour, I said instead, 'You don't have to stay here, you know. Or, you can stay here as long as you like while you look for another job, if that helps.'

He frowned, puzzled, and looked me in the eye then. 'No, I want to be here. I need to be here.'

Before I could ask about that curious phrase, he got up and opened the door.

'Look, I'm sorry I was late. It won't happen again. Now go change for your hike, or you'll be late yourself.'

And with that, I was dismissed.

2

Let me introduce you to my new friend

Still fuming, I pulled on the laces of my hiking boots. Now they were too tight and that made me even madder. He couldn't tell me what to do! I ought to fire him. Throw him out, as I should have done the day he showed up on my doorstep. Why hadn't I told him so? Now it was my own fault he was still there, on my couch, above my studio. Gah! Ordering me around. On this of all days!

That was it. I was going to give him a piece of my mind. Yanking the loops of my laces tight, I stomped out the door and across the courtyard, back to my studio. But just as I was about to enter, I heard voices on the other side of the large wooden doors that led to my driveway. Marie and my mother. And another voice I didn't recognise.

I glared at the door to my studio, but my fight with Thibault would have to wait. Instead, I gathered all my anger and indignation into one sticky, dark thought and pulled it from my head with my thumb and middle finger. My forefinger was too good for that job. The imaginary grossness needed another pull before I could let go of it, but once I'd hurled it across the valley, I felt better, ready to go on my walk.

'Hi, Maman,' I said as I pulled the front door shut behind me, patting the lion's head door knob that lived in the centre of the door before turning to kiss my mother, who looked every bit the mature lady rambler in her stylish yet comfortable clothes.

'Bonjour, Juju. Let me introduce you to my new friend, Chloé Walkure. She loves hiking too, so I invited her. I hope you don't mind.'

'Of course not. The more the merrier.' I held my hand out to the mid-life businesswoman in hiking boots. 'Julie Belmain.' Though what she was wearing was perfectly appropriate, her entire being exuded that commanding air, from her sleek, ash-blonde bob to her red haute couture purse to her brand new, expensive boots.

She took my hand with a firm grip and an open smile. 'It's a pleasure to meet you. Your mother has been telling me what a success you are.'

As we set off on the path that led up the hill on the other side of the road towards my best friend Tiana's house, I hooked my arm around Marie's by way of greeting and, frankly, for support, because Chloé's presence carried a substantial force. 'Oh, well, you know... She is my mother.' The nervous laugh that came out of my mouth annoyed me. Today of all days, I would not be intimidated! By anyone. I straightened and lifted my chin. 'But I am doing quite well. My photography business is bringing in more clients than I can take on, and the hotel I co-own is set to open in two weeks. It's quite exciting.'

And so much work. Jeanette handled pretty much everything – though I suspected Théo, the chef at the café, supported her more than she realised behind the scenes. Still, there were plenty of things she needed my decision or signature on. Service at the café had suffered somewhat, leaving my mother to deal with the usual village grouches complaining about everything, but on the whole, people were looking forward to the new venue opening.

'Well, two weeks if there aren't any more murders to solve.' Marie chuckled, but Maman looked sour.

'That's no way to start a conversa—'

'Murders? Plural? In such a small village?' Chloé panted slightly coming up the steep path. 'I would have thought nothing ever happened here. Isn't that why they built the Centre de Prédiction way out here? For the peaceful surroundings?'

I didn't care for the emphasis she put on that 'way'. When I'd left for the city in the valley, I'd thought Saint-Maurice remote too. Now that I was back, I knew it was exactly the right distance from everywhere. I wanted to tell her so, but my mother, always the mayor, stepped in.

'That's right. Our community is a very tight-knit one, but we pride ourselves on being open to new people and new opportunities. I'm sure I speak for the people in Blacenas, too, when I say that. Like everywhere else, we have our share of unpleasantness, but the real shocker was the discovery of a long lost work of art.'

You could almost see the cloud of pride that hung around my mother. Trust her to turn my business venture into a communal win.

'Ah, yes, I heard about that. Considered putting in a bid, actually. For the novelty value, *tu sais*? But I'm over the Figuration Libre, really. New Objectivity has much more depth to it, don't you agree?'

In the interest of the village, my mother would agree to anything. Chloé prattled on about early twentieth-century art movements while we passed Tiana's house. I peered into the windows, but she'd probably be in her study on the other side of the house, typing away on her latest romance novel.

The path between our houses cut through a copse, the trees obscuring the view over the Saône valley. From here upwards, the hill was still too steep for vineyards, but the rocky surface also allowed fewer trees to grow, meaning whenever we took a moment to catch our breath, we could turn and take in miles and miles of green land, adorned by the shimmering ribbon of the Saône River and bordered in the distance by the mighty, snow-capped Alps.

'Wasn't Jacqueline supposed to join us?' Marie asked. We'd been quicker coming up the hill than the other two, allowing us to avoid knowing how much pricey art Chloé had accumulated.

'Yes, but she texted me that she was running late and would join at the statue.'

The statue was a giant, white Mary at the top of the hill. La Dame de Saint-Maurice watched over the village, but was herself watched over by the Vicomtesse de Montmales, who lived in the big château over on the next hill.

'Your mother tells me you're quite the artist as well.' Chloé was panting rather heavily when she caught up, and we were only halfway up the hill. 'I'm afraid I haven't taken the time to look up your work, but it sounds intriguing. Do you simply take the pictures, or is there some artistic input involved?'

I groaned inwardly. I hadn't come across too many supporters of it, fortunately, but I'd heard the idea before: photography only captures reality, so it can't be art. 'My camera only captures the end result, of course, but it's all the work that goes into capturing that image that makes it art. And not all art has to make you feel sad, it just has to make you feel,' I added as a precaution. I'd had this conversation with Tiana too. Romance novels couldn't be art, because they weren't 'deep' enough, didn't make you think about the so-called bigger things in life. As if only the solemn and serious things in life could be big. Though we both agreed not all writing, nor all photographs, were art, that didn't automatically make the opposite true.

'Fascinating,' Chloé declared, and surprisingly, I believed her. Though she was concentrating on the path in front of her, which now included small boulders to be scaled, there wasn't a hint of sarcasm in her voice. 'What inspires you to take the pictures you take? It's a kind of... boudoir style?'

Marie struck up a conversation with my mother, so I could explore this unexpected side of my mother's 'new friend'. The path narrowed as we neared the top of the hill, so I took the lead instead of us walking side by side. 'I suppose there are similarities, but no, my style is more tongue-in-cheek, focussed on the colourful and fun instead of the seductive aspect.'

'Ah, to show—'

I turned round at the sound of stones skidding down the hill and grabbed Chloé's hand to balance her.

'Thanks. To show a woman who's comfortable in her own body, you mean?'

I blinked. 'Exactly.' It didn't happen very often that I completely misjudged people, but she blew me away with that remark. After her dismissal of an art style as lacking in depth, I'd placed her among the *blah blah blah* crowd, saying whatever they thought was The Thing To Say, which often included the words 'too commercial', 'too mainstream', or 'unoriginal'. Because although art is in the eye of the beholder, they were obviously the best beholders, the more equal animals. But Chloé now showed an insight that set her apart from that group.

As I turned with a big grin to continue on the path, I resolved to look up her business when I got home. I might get the chance to ask her before then, but we'd reached La Dame, and Jacqueline distracted me by folding me into a giant hug.

'I haven't seen you in ages!' she squeaked into my ear, making me wince. Jacqueline, a policewoman through and through, wasn't usually this exuberant, so I giggled in surprise.

She wrinkled her nose. 'You're giggling.'

'You're squeaking,' I retorted.

Then we both laughed as she threw up her hands. 'Yeah, well, I have a day off, the sun is shining, I'm seeing my friend... What more could I want?'

'You're right, you have every reason to be happy.' Though I'd seen her happy before, and this was one step further. I suspected she'd received some kind of good news, but if she felt like it, she'd tell me later. 'Which way are we going? Up towards Montmales or across to Blacenas?'

'Oh, I promised Chloé we'd take her partway back to the Centre,' my mother said with a little wave to Jacqueline.

'Blacenas it is. Jacquie, this is Chloé Walkure.' I inclined my head to Chloé. 'I didn't realise you were staying at the Centre de Prédiction.' I made it sound like a question, since yet again, I hadn't expected someone so seemingly grounded to stay at such a hip and... well... frivolous venue.

'It's good to meet you, Jacqueline. Shall we?' Chloé steered us after my mother and Marie, who had already taken the path downhill towards Blacenas. 'I think it's important to keep broadening my horizon,' she added to me once we set off. 'I spent this morning in a floatation tank, for instance, which I'd never experienced before. We meet so many of the same people in the same circumstances, that whenever we travel somewhere new, we like to stay in a kind of place we haven't tried yet.'

'We?' Maybe I was being too curious, but she shouldn't have mentioned another person if she wasn't willing to elaborate.

'My personal assistant, Wylène Chiche, always comes with me. She is an absolute treasure. Young, but so competent. I honestly don't know what I'd do without her. She's wise beyond her age, and we see eye to eye on almost everything. She's been with me for almost five years, and I hope she'll never leave. Truly.'

Jacqueline pulled down the corners of her mouth in appreciation. 'High praise.'

I nodded. 'That's wonderful. Assistants that good are hard to find.' Didn't I know it.

Jacqueline, apparently, was done with the subject. She closed her eyes and inhaled deeply through her nose. 'I just love that April smell. Finally some real warmth, real flowers coming through. Not just those overly ambitious spring flowers that trick you into thinking winter is gone. Real flowers, with scent.'

For Jacqueline, that was quite the display of emotion, and I grinned. 'I didn't know you were so passionate about flowers. I'm seeing a whole new side of you.'

'Don't get used to it.' Her tone was serious, but she winked while she said it.

The path, that had gone down as we moved away from La Dame, now took a steep turn onto the next hill, and we were quiet for a while as we concentrated on the rocks beneath our feet. When the trail levelled out at a clearing, my mother held her pace to walk next to me.

'Did you look at that recipe I sent you? This time of year—'

She was interrupted by Jacqueline's phone.

'That's not a very peaceful sound,' Marie remarked as she stood and took in the view over the Saône valley. Gazing out at the Alps in the far distance was one of my favourite pastimes, so I joined her while Jacqueline first groaned, then grumbled, then sighed dramatically, and finally growled while thrusting her phone back into her pocket.

'I have to work. Can you believe it? My one day off, and some idiot has to kill herself.'

I winced at her casual words.

'There must be others who can take over?' my mother asked.

'Our team isn't that big. We don't ordinarily need more than three homicide detectives in Villefranche, but one is on sick leave, and the other apparently got called out to something else this morning. I'm sorry, *les filles*, but I'll have to go.'

'Actually, the quickest way down from here is to follow the trail we were already on.' I pointed to the edge of the clearing. 'Or is your car on the other side?'

'It is, but you're right, that way is quicker.' She set off with long strides, making the rest of us scamper to keep up.

'But if your car is that way... Unless... Where are you going?' I knew the answer before she gave it and glanced over my shoulder at Marie, who looked back in alarm.

'Centre de Prédiction.'

3

How dare he?

Jessica Rose rammed her fist into the clay. Sculpting could be therapeutic at the best of times, but right now, she needed its calming powers badly. She couldn't remember ever being this angry. How dare he? How *dare* he! Another punch, and the clay went flying off the table.

Jessica blinked at the innocent, misshapen blob on the floor, contemplating the wisdom of a certain action only after the fact, as usual. But this time, not even sculpting would do the trick. It just reminded her of *him*. Growling, she stomped out of her studio to wash her hands and take off her apron. She'd thought to turn her raging emotion into a masterpiece, but unless the masterpiece was chunks of clay thrown at a wall, today was not the day she'd be making it.

He would probably say the wall was now art. *He* would steal it, sell it for some exorbitant amount, and she'd have to have a new wall built. Anything and everything was money to him. And now he was stealing her thoughts. She didn't want to think about *him*. He was making her think about him. The utter toilet brush!

Snatching her keys off the hook by the door, she made her way to her blue and white Citroën, a jaunty 2CV Charleston. Her best friend, the one she could give free reign and trust that it would take care of her. If the world conspired against her and her art, an hour or so driving around and talking to her friend would always give her perspective. Not to mention it had brought her places she would otherwise never have thought to go. Just sliding behind the wheel and starting up the engine already made her feel better. She would go left, away from the city, and see where her friend would take her.

Her friend took her back to the city. That was the only place this road led. Jessica had been enjoying the soft spring sunlight on all the bright splashes of yellows and pinks and greens against the remaining dull brown of winter, turning left and right at crossroads without thinking, but now irritation stabbed at her new-found peace.

'Yes, I know I'm hungry, but I have plenty of food at home.'

Annoyingly, the car said nothing.

'All right, so I don't necessarily want to go home.'

Understandably, the car said nothing.

'I think I have an energy bar here somewhere, actually.' She rummaged around in the glove compartment but her hand found nothing but car papers, sketches on the back of gas receipts, and empty wrappers.

She frowned. 'I'm sure...' Taking her eyes off the road for one second, she glanced at the mess and immediately located the elusive snack. Triumphantly, she held it up to the world, gasped, and slammed on the brakes.

Inches from her bumper stood a man, looking less than impressed at her proximity. Apart from a raised eyebrow, though, you wouldn't have thought from his appearance that she'd just almost hit him with her car. With a backpack slung over one shoulder, his stance was confident, or perhaps – well, almost certainly, under the circumstances – overconfident.

While her pounding heart slowly made way for other sounds to reach her ears, he cocked his head, probably waiting for her to apologise. Well, he could wait for her limbs to remember they could move first. Moulding her open mouth into a sheepish smile, Jessica showed him the energy bar by way of explanation, mouthing 'sorry'. She expected him to either start yelling at her or dismiss her as a silly female. These handsome, arrogant types usually did. Instead, he gave her a forgiving smile. Condescending, yes, but it was enough to make her want to apologise. She pulled out the handbrake from the dashboard of her classic car, shut off the engine, and got out, still clutching her snack as she leaned over the door.

'I'm so sorry. Wasn't looking. *Évidemment.*' She waved the bar around and suddenly felt exactly the silly female she'd never been when viewed as such.

The man's smile had turned curious, but his mouth remained closed. No insults, nor acknowledgement.

'Are you okay? Where were you going? Can I give you a lift?' It was the least she could do, even though he was going in the opposite direction. Where *was* he going? With those shoes, though sturdy and practical enough, he wasn't out hiking. But this road didn't lead anywhere worth going for miles. In fact, the first thing he'd come across was her studio, and after that another bunch of nothing for a long while.

'Nowhere.' His deep voice surprised her.

'Excuse me?'

'I was going nowhere in particular.'

Huh. Interesting. 'Anywhere but there, *hein*? I guess we have that in common.'

Again, he didn't answer, but his eyes joined in with the smile. Now that her first shock had worn off, she could see that he was, in fact, exceptionally good-looking. Black hair, dark eyes, straight nose, strong chin – he had it all. In her mind, she was already modelling him from clay.

The wind blowing her long, flowery skirt against his black jeans had her stepping back, and she realised she'd been staring at him. 'So, err...' She pointed up the hill to try and recover some dignity. 'You're on the right road to nowhere. But if you want to go past nowhere to somewhere with an ounce of potential, I can take you there?'

He narrowed his eyes. 'I thought you were going the other way.'

'Oh, no. Well, yes, but that was just my car. I was going nowhere too, really.'

The handsome stranger laughed, finally defrosting a little, and pointed up the hill too. 'Anywhere but there? Where I was going?'

'It's complicated. Do you want a lift or not?'

'Yes. Let's go nowhere together.'

Not until that exact moment had Jessica realised she was inviting an strange man into a very enclosed space with her. Was this wise?

The man opened the passenger door and stretched his hand out over the roof of the little car. 'I'm Alain. Alain Coquard. And you are' – he dropped his hand to the fabric – 'having second thoughts.'

Shaking her auburn curls, Jessica hurried to take Alain's hand. 'No, it's all right. Jessica Rose. Let's go.' It *was* all right. Her friend would protect her. Although, she really should have considered just how close the passenger sat to the driver in a 2CV.

Alain put his backpack between his legs and made himself comfortable. He didn't seem to be getting ready to kill or maim, so Jessica told herself to relax, started the car, and turned it around.

After ten minutes of polite conversation that had Jessica tell half her life story in a vain attempt to find out more about him, Alain sat up. 'What's that?'

The only structure in sight was an ugly concrete building on an overgrown plot of land. The windows were still intact but covered in dust and dirt. The garage doors on the side showed big patches of rust and probably hadn't been opened in years. The only thing alleviating the dreariness of the place were some swirly, metal letters naming the building: À La Rose Des Vents.

'Abandoned car dealership.'

'Compass rose... Didn't you say your name was Jessica Rose? Let's go there.'

Jessica stared at him in disbelief. 'That's where you see potential?'

He shrugged. 'We'll see. Are you sure it's abandoned?'

'Well, yes. Apart from the bit in the back where my studio is.'

Alain turned to her and flashed a knowing grin. 'I knew it had potential. Would you mind showing me?'

She hesitated. Was she really going to let a strange man into her home? But before she could answer herself, her friend had already taken the turn. Some friend.

4

We're here with you

'Do you know who died?' My heart was racing, and only partly because we were hurrying down a hilly path.

'Yes.' Jacqueline was already in full policewoman mode.

'It's not Moira, is it?' Please don't let it be Moira.

Jacqueline frowned slightly, and my heart sank. 'Who's Moira? But no.'

I had to stop walking to catch my breath, putting my hand over my heart to calm it down. I could see the relief flooding Marie's face as well.

My mother and Chloé caught up to us. 'What's going on?' *Maman* asked, putting a hand on my arm with a concerned frown.

I took a big breath and started down the path once more. 'Someone died at the Centre de Prédiction, but it's not Moira.'

'What?' Only when Chloé spoke did I remember she also knew someone at the Centre. 'Who?'

'I – I don't know. But Jacqueline said "kill herself",' I added quickly. 'Your assistant was happy, right?'

'Yes.' Chloé closed her eyes and let out a breath. 'Yes, she would never kill herself. When you said 'died', you had me worried for a second. Ha! I think I'm starting to rely on her a bit too much. She's a little too focussed on her looks, you know, being so young, but I literally wouldn't know what to do without her.'

Marie joined us after giving up on staying with Jacqueline. 'Wow, that woman can walk. I thought I'd keep her company, but she took off like a Bugatti.'

'Strange, if you think about it,' Chloé said. 'The woman is already dead. What's the hurry?'

'I think we should be grateful that we're able to enjoy life,' my mother said. 'Our own, and the new life sprouting all around us.'

We followed the trail at a leisurely pace, each of us engrossed in our own thoughts. New life sounded great. I'd much rather appreciate the young leaves on old branches, the soft squeaks coming from a nest above us, and the smiles of my friends that were lively and new each time, despite being so familiar. Life was good. My mother and Marie had produced it. I had found it when I set up my studio here in Saint-Maurice.

And yet, on this day, life was exactly what was bringing me down. Yes, the death of that poor woman was a tragedy, but I didn't know her. No, my mother's words put someone else in my mind. Someone I did know, whether I wanted to or not. Exactly four years ago today, my ex-husband Franck had been sent to prison. Before they led him away, he'd looked me straight in the eyes and said, 'Enjoy life, *mon amour*. In four years, it'll be over.'

Suddenly cold all over, I shuddered, right at the moment both my mother and Marie hooked their arms through mine.

'We're here with you,' Marie said with a smile. She had not been there four years ago, but she knew what had happened.

Maman squeezed my arm. 'Not going anywhere. You have a lot more life to enjoy.'

I swallowed. Neither of them would ever know how much their support meant to me at that moment. I would never again feel as alone as I had done four years ago. Today, I wouldn't even have the time. Tiana, amazing friend that she was, had hired the village's *salle des fêtes* for the afternoon and invited all the people that cared about me. When she'd announced this to me, I'd thought the hall would be far too big for such a modest company, but wherever I'd gone, people had told me they were looking forward to the party. People like Hanna, the woman who ran the supermarket, or André and Tino, the village gardeners, whom I'd only started to notice after Monsieur Durand greeted them on his way to the *boulangerie*. I had been back in the village for less than a year, but already these people had become dear to me. And to my utter surprise, the feeling had been mutual.

My heart had been singing with that feeling, but now that the day had come, my mind kept wandering to that other event of the day. Franck would be released at three o'clock this afternoon, and I knew, even though I'd be surrounded by friends, I'd be staring at the clock, wondering if he'd be thinking about me too.

I hugged my mother and friend to my sides as we exited the forest, determined not to let the rest of the day be spoiled as well. The Centre de Prédiction stretched out before us. It was an odd building, standing out against the rolling landscape of vineyards with its moss green glass walls and organic shapes. On one end it looked like a crashing wave. On the other, it was almost like cupped hands holding a shiny, golden ball. The ball in question was large enough to contain a sizeable room, but as I'd never been inside, I didn't know if it was actually accessible. I imagined it would be pitch black in there, so it might not work as a room to begin with.

I'd seen the building before, passing it on walks mostly, but ordinarily it looked relatively peaceful. Now, frowning people were running in and out, some wearing suits, some wearing white coveralls, some wearing bathrobes. The robed people huddled together, glancing over their shoulders and speaking in hushed tones.

As we approached, Chloé began to fidget, despite her earlier assurance. I inserted myself into one of the little robed groups, adopting the same conspiratorial posture.

'Isn't it awful?'

Nodding all around.

'Unbelievable,' whispered a woman with an aubergine bob.

'Such a shame,' acknowledged a tall man with wavy grey hair and a grey moustache.

They'd accepted me without doubt. Watching Beau the past few months had taught me a thing or two about acting, and I felt rather pleased about that. 'Do they know what happened yet?' I asked.

'I heard she drank drain cleaner.' The bobbed woman grimaced.

'I thought it was lye,' a short, blondish grey woman who'd been quiet up till then remarked.

Bobbed woman huffed. 'Where would she have got *that*? You read too many old books. I keep telling you to watch that show – what's it called?'

Grey man addressed me. 'As far as I know, she stabbed herself in the gut.'

'No she didn't!' the others harmonised.

'Then where did all the blood come from?'

'I only meant,' I interrupted before this conversation could get any more graphic, 'do they know who? And why?'

'Well, yes, obviously. It was that Chiche girl. Madeleine? Mylène? That was the first thing we knew.' Aubergine pulled up an eyebrow, finally realising she didn't actually know me. 'Who are you, anyway?'

The shorter woman stared wistfully past me. 'Does anyone ever really know why?'

'Just passing by,' I offered by way of explanation, while I stepped backwards in retreat, rejoining my mother and Marie with Aubergine's stares pricking in my back. Chloé had already separated from them and was talking to one of the police people. As I watched her, she collapsed, the policewoman barely able to catch her.

'Oh no,' my mother whispered as she hurried towards her friend.

'How? Why?' Chloé wailed, though she didn't seem to hear the policewoman's answer.

I caught the last few words when we were close enough. 'But we're doing everything in our power to find out.'

Maman enveloped Chloé in one of her motherly hugs. I hoped they worked on Chloé as well as they'd always done on me, because the poor woman was shaking so much she could barely stand.

'I don't understand. She was happy. There was nothing wrong. I don't... I...'

My mother shushed her, rocking her gently from side to side. Feeling like an intruder, I turned towards the building, where people were still milling about. One man caught my eye. He was wearing a long, white coat that accentuated his slim figure, making him look taller than he actually was. The garment was something between a lab coat and a Victorian frock coat, which he'd accessorised with a kind of turban-durag combination in white silk. The ensemble was memorable, to say the least. The man came towards us, his hands crossed flat over his chest and his eyebrows drooping. I didn't know if he was trying to express worry, guilt, or concern, but it all looked over-the-top and fake. A lab-coated, twitchy woman with a tight ponytail and dark-rimmed glasses followed him, clutching a tablet to her chest.

'Madame Walkure, you have my deepest sympathy in this hour of dread and despair. Please know that my staff will be at your complete disposal for anything you might desire. Perhaps an EMDR session, or a relaxing hot stone massage?'

Chloé didn't react, but my mother's eyes were unusually cold when she addressed the man. 'Monsieur Othman, while we appreciate your concern, I think what Madame Walkure needs most is some quiet time. I'm sure that can be arranged too.'

'*Bien sur*, we have several facilities for silence therapy that—'

'I meant she should be left alone.'

The man cast down his gaze, performed a small bow, and retreated, his underling scurrying after him.

'You know him?' I asked.

'He's the owner of this... venue. I don't like him.'

She might as well have thrown every insult in the book at him. For my mother to profess a dislike to someone, they must have kicked a whole litter of puppies. Not that she didn't dislike people, but as the mayor of Saint-Maurice, she would generally keep her dislike to herself, not even expressing it to my brother or me.

Chloé took a deep, shuddering breath, and my mother slowly let go. 'I think I'm okay now. It was just... the shock, you know?'

Maman nodded, rubbing Chloé's arms.

'I still don't understand. I don't even know what to do now.' She wiped her wet face with her sleeve, pushing some strands of hair behind her ear.

'I'm sure the police will be able to help with that, but I'm here too. Don't worry.' She turned to me, but kept an arm around Chloé. 'Juju, I'm going to stay here for a while. Why don't you head back, because I don't think you'll be needed.'

I nodded, and with some words of sympathy, Marie and I left. We were quiet most of the way back, save for the mutual agreement that it must be horrible for Chloé. But since we didn't really know her and had never even met her assistant, there really wasn't any more to be said.

'Do you think Jacqueline will be at the party later?' Marie asked.

'I doubt it.' I sighed. Of all the people I would have liked to be there today, Jacquie ranked near the top. She knew the devastation Franck had caused and had been instrumental in turning my life around, though she never wanted that credit. 'Just doing her job.' As always.

'Well, I'm sure it'll be fun nonetheless. I'm going to go change. See you in an hour.' She kissed my cheek and followed the road towards Villefranche, whereas I had to go through the village to get to my house.

Though April was usually warm enough to go out without a coat, the smell of wood fires from people's fireplaces still hung around the village. In the distance, Madame Braymand's house was being torn down. Soon they'd be building their precious apartments there. I passed the school, where Mylène Grasset was singing nursery rhymes with the little ones. Life, such as it was, went on.

Outside the *boulangerie*, Thibault was leaning against the wall, phone in hand. He didn't see me, so I entered the building to buy a baguette to go with my lunch. When I came back out, I expected him to be gone, but he was still there.

'Are you coming, or are you waiting for someone?' The someone usually being Céline, but since I'd bought the baguette from her father just now, I didn't think she'd be in.

He started, too engrossed in what he saw on his screen to notice me before.

'Motorcycles?' I asked with a nod to his phone, which he quickly pocketed.

'No.' We set off home in what I was beginning to consider an uncomfortable silence when we passed the cemetery. On the bench outside the wall were two teenage girls, one comforting the other, who was quietly crying.

'Oh, not more tears,' I said, feeling sorry for the girl, but also for myself. I'd felt like crying since I woke up, but I'd told myself I was now a strong woman and I wasn't going to let Franck rule my life any more. It had worked up till now, but all these sad people weren't helping.

Beau didn't respond. All he said was, 'You don't need me this afternoon, do you?'

My head snapped towards him. 'What do you mean? You're not coming to the party?'

He rubbed his neck. 'I kind of... have a thing.'

Frowning, I halted, which made him stop, too, after a few steps. 'I kind of do, too, you know. This is important to me.'

He stared into the distance behind me, rolling his shoulder and bobbing his head. 'I know, but... I'm already with you all the time.'

And this was his explanation for why he couldn't be here now? When I actually wanted him there and wasn't thinking of ways to kick him out?

'So are you, like, *leaving* leaving? I have a shoot the day after tomorrow, and I was counting on you.' Like I was this morning, but I thought it best not to mention that now. Was he really going to leave on this of all days?

'What? No! I'm just going to Jessica's.'

'Jessica?' What Jessica in my mental contact list had any connection to Thibault?

'Jessica Rose? You went to her exposition after she saved your super expensive ugly mural.'

'Oh, that Jessica. Why are you going there?' Instead of to the party where you're supposed to be?

Rubbing his neck again, he stared at his feet this time, kicking at the asphalt. 'She asked me to model for her.'

My head shot forward several inches, my eyes bulging and my jaw dropping. It was all I could do to stop myself shouting, 'What?!'

'So you'll model for her, but not for me?' I squeaked instead.

He frowned at the ground. 'It's different. She's a real artist. She makes classical art. Hers is objective. Your pictures are... suggestive. They make me feel leered at.'

He still wouldn't look at me, but all my indignation deflated. 'My clients love them,' I said in a small voice. My pictures were supposed to be fun. A little tongue-in-cheek, but not degrading. The opposite, in fact. The woman signing up for my pictures felt in control and confident. How could it not have that effect on Beau?

'They choose to do them,' was all he offered.

So, I was beneath him. My eyebrows came together in a thunderstorm frown. 'And I choose to let you stay. I don't ask all that much in return. Wouldn't want to spoil your impeccable reputation.'

What I meant was the party, but he took it to mean a photo shoot.

'I don't want to do it, all right? *Je file.*'

Before I could answer, he'd stalked off, back towards the village.

'Who needs you!'

Well, I did. But then, I didn't. I held my chin high. I was a strong woman who wasn't going to let Franck rule my life any more. Or Beau. Men in general!

I stomped towards my house, muttering to myself like a silly old witch. 'You're a terrible model. Couldn't use any of those pictures. And I know you printed and framed that one on your bike! Even though you hide it when I come over. *Leered at.* You should know.'

I hadn't even asked him to model. We just had that one session way back in October in exchange for letting him stay, but he hadn't listened to my direction at all. Being Beau, he looked beautiful in all of the pictures, but they weren't representative of my style and brand at all, so I'd had no use for them. Unsurprisingly, I hadn't pushed for more.

But now he was willingly modelling for a sculptor! What did she have that I didn't? According to him, class. Ha! I knew how she worked. She'd told me herself. Yes, she was classically trained, but the stuff she liked to make, the torsos I imagined Beau would be modelling for, didn't sell. One day, out of frustration, she'd made an angry, abstract sculpture with lots of spikes, and her boyfriend at the time, who owned a gallery, had displayed it. Boom! Instant fame and fortune. Now she only made the spiky stuff and reserved the figurative art for herself. Which means she'd essentially be the only one who'd be looking at Beau, even after he'd been turned into a sculpture. Is that what he wanted? Exclusivity? Not if the grapevine was to be believed.

I sighed. Why did I even care? Beau could do as he pleased, and I had nothing to say about it. I put my finger and thumb to my temple and pulled out as much of the negativity as I could.

It helped me let Beau's choices be his own. But it still stung that he chose Jessica Rose's art over mine.

5

It has potential

She'd shown him around the entire empty showroom and now Jessica was desperate for some lunch. She'd had an emotional morning, and even her car had sent her towards town to get some food. But Alain was inspecting the place as if he were thinking of moving in. Most of the building was dirty and dusty, as Jessica kept the doors to the large showroom closed. She'd only ever used the back room where she'd set up her studio, as well as the small kitchen and even smaller bathroom, and the office area where she'd managed to fit in a single bed. One corner of her studio held a couch and a couple of beanbags where she relaxed at the end of the day, but though the front of the building looked out over the Saône valley, she never set foot in there.

'What exactly are you looking for?'

'Nothing in particular,' he answered as he ran his hand over a window stile.

Helpful.

'I'm starting a new project, so I want to know if this venue will accommodate that.'

'All right, well, I'm going to heat up some leftovers. Hope you weren't looking for a big steak dinner, because I'm a vegetarian. There's artichoke tagine and *zaalouk*, aubergine salad.'

'Fine,' he said, but then he turned with a dazzling smile that made her stomach tingle. *'Merci.'*

She returned an uncertain grin, retreating as fast as she could. *Ugh!* Handsome men were so frustrating. As much as she told herself it's what inside that matters, one smile from a handsome man and she was all aflutter.

She busied herself preparing the meal and setting her tiny kitchen table for two. The fact that she actually had two clean plates surprised her even more than the fact that this table would hold two plates. She never had people over. Even her ex-boyfriend never stayed long enough to have a meal here. That should have tipped her off, maybe, but she hadn't noticed at the time. Too handsome. She rolled her eyes at herself.

'Smells good.' Alain wandered in, putting a tape measure in his backpack.

Jessica couldn't help feeling like she did in her car, that this space put her in too close a proximity to the good-looking stranger. 'Thanks. So what do you think?' She was dying to know what he could have in mind, measuring a dusty old building he'd randomly come across.

Alain leisurely pulled back a chair and sat at the table, leaning back as if he owned the place. But he shot back up when the pointy leaves of her thriving sansevieria plant poked his back. Turning around, he pointed his thumb at the plant in the corner and arched an eyebrow. 'I don't think it wants me here.'

'Sorry.' Jessica delivered her sheepish grin again. 'Nobody ever sits there. I'll move it.'

She moved towards him, but he held up his hand, pushed the chair out of the way, and picked up the enormous pot. She had to retreat and lean backwards against the kitchen counter to let him pass.

'I've never seen a sansevieria this big,' his voice came from between the leaves.

'It lives on coffee.' Was he going to tell her what he was doing here? Other than that she'd brought him. 'You'll have to fill up your plate here at the stove. As you can see, there's no more room on the table.' If he thought he was being mysterious by keeping so quiet as he moved around, he was dead wrong. Though nothing he did was necessarily suspicious, his silence was making Jessica nervous. 'Are you always this much of a talker?'

He looked up from filling his plate and blinked, eyebrows raised. Then a burst of laughter bounced around the little kitchen. 'I'm sorry. I was thinking about the building.' He took a seat across from her and pinned her with a mischievous glance. 'It has potential.'

Berating herself yet again for feeling her freckles burn, Jessica took a big bite of her *zaalouk*. 'You're not going to turn out to be a creepy serial killer, are you?'

His eyes gleamed with a wide smile. 'No, that is not one of my aspirations. Though, of course, I would say that if I were a killer.'

She chose to ignore that last remark. 'Good, because I have enough trouble with a backstabbing ex.'

Oh no. Did she just mention her ex? Strangely, Alain wasn't running for the door. Instead, he took another bite.

'Hm, this is really good.' Alain nodded while pointing his fork at his plate.

'It's Moroccan. Family recipe.' She wasn't much of a cook, but the few things her mother had managed to teach her were firm favourites. All too aware of his knees touching hers under the table, she tried to keep her mind otherwise engaged. 'Potential for what, though?'

All he did was shrug. 'Do you own the building?'

That was such a ludicrous question that she snorted in a very unladylike manner and instantly regretted it. *Let the handsome man see your good side*, the girly part of her said. *And what exactly is my good side*, her feminist part retorted. She went with that and pursed her lips. 'What do *you* think? My art may be good, but it's only because of my dealer that I make any money at all. *He's* the one who owns the building.'

'He's into art *and* property management?'

Jessica rolled her eyes. 'What isn't he into? Property, art, tech, energy, cryptocurrency… Anything that will make him money, basically. That's all he cares about. And don't think he's guided by any scruples at all.'

Alain leaned back in his chair. 'Sounds like you should find someone else to represent you.'

'Yeah!' It came out in another inelegant snort, but Jessica was still too angry with her ex-dealer to care. 'Well, I made sure of that only this morning.'

An amused smile played around Alain's lips. 'Good. I'll make sure not to mention you when I ask him about the lease for the showroom.'

All of Jessica's anger froze. All of her thoughts froze too. She only remembered to breathe after a few long seconds, when Alain frowned in concern. 'I… didn't think of that.'

He gave a slight head shake. 'Think of what?'

'He's going to kick me out.' Her heart unfroze with a vengeance and started hammering in her chest. 'I- I'm only here because he couldn't find anyone to take the building off his hands, and I was making him money. Now that I effectively fired him, I'll be homeless.'

'I'm sure it won't come to that.' Alain sat up and reached for her, but apparently thought better of it and rested his hand on the edge of the table instead. 'Did he say anything about it this morning?'

'No, but—'

'Then we'll figure something out. If I don't make an offer, he'll have no other use for the building, so why not let you stay?'

'Oh, I can tell you don't know him.' She let out a shaky laugh. 'He's vindictive. Spiteful. That's exactly why I got rid of him. If he has the power to ruin me, he will use it. And he has it.' By now, Jessica was on the verge of tears. Her mind was racing through all kinds of outrageous possibilities, discarding one straw after another until there was nothing left to clutch.

'Well... then... I will make him an offer and I'll make sure you get to stay. How about that? If money is the most important thing to him, my offer must be worth more than getting back at you?'

It took a few moments for Jessica's thoughts to focus. This might be more than a straw. It looked like a log. But even if it was only an inflatable one, it might keep her adrift. 'Can you do that? Why would you do that?'

He smiled and spread his arm over the empty plates. 'You gave me lunch. One kindness deserves another.'

That statement was so directly in contrast with the attitude of the nasty man who had occupied her thoughts all day that it made her laugh. If nothing else, it broke her unhelpful spiral of emotions. 'Thanks. That helps. But seriously, could you...?' She didn't want to finish the sentence. Could you spend that amount of money on me? Could you please go to my ex-dealer-cum-current-unofficial-landlord and make sure I won't be out on the street come tomorrow?

'I think you don't have to worry about losing your studio just yet.' Though he kept his gaze down, she was all too happy to accept the words. What other option did she have? 'I'll wash, you dry?'

'Oh! Thanks, yes.' Taking a clean tea towel from the cupboard, Jessica watched the strange man from the corner of her eye as he rinsed the plates and filled the sink with soapy water. As little as she knew about him, he was quickly starting to feel more familiar than Xavier ever had. Xavier was at home in fancy restaurants where she felt out of place. Alain, whatever it was he did, seemed to be at home in her tiny, cheap kitchen. Yet his backpack and shoes looked expensive.

Could he really be the solution to her problem? She took a plate from him and dried it. Worry wasn't going to help her, but was she really going to depend on yet another man to get her out of trouble? On the other hand, she hadn't come up with anything useful herself. She hadn't even thought about the repercussions of her actions. She knew she should have got something in writing. But then, she'd torn up her agreement in front of him, so that would probably have voided her living arrangements as well. Rash decisions, as usual. But she had literally seen red when he—

The door to the little kitchen opened and Beau entered. What was he doing here? *Oh! Right!* He was here to model for her. With everything else going on, that had completely slipped her mind.

Beau hesitated when he saw Alain. 'Hi. You said half past twelve, right?'

A glance at the oven clock told her it was twenty-five past. 'Yes, yes, no problem, come in. We're still having a bit of a *sieste*. This is Alain.' She turned to Alain. 'Beau, my model for the day.'

Alain held up his hand in greeting. 'Hi. Don't mind me, I won't be in the way. I have some business to tend to.' He gave Jessica a quick wink that squeezed her stomach.

Unable to decide whether she liked the sensation, she said, 'Yes, but not before dessert. Have a seat, Beau. Do you want some? It's crème brûlée. Store-bought, I'm afraid.'

For some reason, Beau had gone from uncertain to smug. He leaned against the door frame, his arms folded over his chest and his legs crossed. 'No, thanks. I've had lunch. I'll just wait here.'

Whatever he was thinking, she had the distinct feeling he was making fun of her somehow. She eyed him suspiciously, but the look she got back was all innocence. When she'd met him at her expo a few months back, he'd been there with Julie Belmain, whom she'd met under curious circumstances to do with Julie's new hotel and had only talked to a handful of times since. But Thibault had asked all kinds of interested questions about Jessica's work, so they'd kept in touch. He'd shown her some of his drawings, she'd introduced him to some of her artist friends, and at some point she'd dared to ask him if he'd model for her. The ease with which he'd agreed had made her wonder why she hadn't asked sooner, but not everyone was so willing to shed their clothes.

'Julie plays this song too,' Beau said, pointing at the radio softly playing The Hollies. He hummed along for a few bars, then sang, 'Then she played with all the boys and free sex. What's the attraction in what they're doing?'

Jessica laughed. 'Sure, that works. It's "older boys and prefects",' she explained to Alain at his raised eyebrows.

'You like old music?' he asked.

'My mother does. I grew up with this stuff. I tune into this station when I need to calm down.'

'Your accent,' Alain suddenly said. 'You're not from around here, are you?'

At least he packaged it nicely. Usually it was the colour of her skin that made people ask. Her Moroccan ancestors had left her with a freckled tan and dark copper curls. And when she answered 'I grew up in Marseille', she would often get the I-knew-it nod.

Alain, however, arched his eyebrows. 'And you left? Don't most artists go there instead?'

'Not to where I'm from. People there don't appreciate the artist, even if they might like the art.' She glanced at Beau, who grinned. She'd had this conversation with him too. 'I know, a lot of people are drawn to the Provence region, Aix and Arles, but I found inspiration in the vineyards of the Beaujolais. Even though I don't do landscape.'

She shrugged. 'Inspiration' sounded better than 'someone who wanted to sell my stuff'. She handed Alain some crème brûlée and turned to throw away the packaging, when there was a loud knock on the door.

Beau opened it, but had to step back when a short but burly black man pushed his way inside.

'Jessica Rose?'

Tentatively, Jessica raised her hand. 'That's me.'

'What is your relation to Xavier Grosse?'

'Excuse me, but... who are you?'

He held up a badge. 'Brigadier-chef Étienne Chagrin. Answer the question, please.'

'He's my ex. He also sells my art and he owns this building.' From the corner of her eye, she saw Alain and Beau exchange glances, which irked her. So her life was a bit complicated right now. Had they never had weird relationships? And why was this police officer in her kitchen exposing her weird relationship?

'Where were you between nine and ten this morning?'

Jessica straightened her shoulders. The frown that had started when she witnessed the exchange between Beau and Alain deepened. 'Since you're asking me those two questions together, I assume you already know I was in Xavier's office. What's all this about?'

'He's dead.'

6

You're the star of the party

Pacing back and forth between the full-length mirror and my wardrobe, I couldn't decide on what to wear to this blasted party. I'd changed from the red silk to the green lace and back half a dozen times already, but now I was considering the yellow polka dots.

There was only one thing for it. I grabbed my phone and video-called my best friend. Tiana was not at her house. That painting in the background depicted the *vendanges*, the grape picking at the end of the season, and had been the pride of some local artist when it was picked to be displayed in the *salle des fêtes*. It made sense that Tiana would be there, since she was organising the blasted party. But why didn't she look half as stressed as I was feeling right now?

'How dressed-up am I meant to be?'

'Knowing you, you're overdressed already.' Tiana was joined by her neighbour Catherine, who gave me a happy wave in the camera.

But that answer wasn't helping me at all. Why couldn't she just tell me what to wear? She knew every single item in my wardrobe, for crying out loud. I growled at her.

At that point Tiana's boyfriend, an American named Lucas, came into view, peering at his own phone. 'That sounds like how I feel. It's weird. I've been in France for over five years now, and I still expect it to be true when a website says something will be delivered within ten days...'

Catherine giggled at this. But then, she almost always giggled when Lucas was present. We'd all got used to it by now. Even Catherine's partner Daniel had given up looking up from his paper about it. Tiana and I had tried to find out what it was about Lucas that set Catherine off. It wasn't just that he was handsome. We'd sent Beau in as a test, but he only came back with a plate of cookies. Maybe he was too young. Then we'd invited her and my brother David to dinner, but even though my brother had dialled down his usual haughty air for Her Bubbliness, the giggles remained reserved for Lucas. Our investigation was ongoing.

'Good to see you, Lucas,' Catherine fawned. 'I always knew you two would be good together. I'm so glad I had a helping hand in that.' Lucas smiled at her, and Catherine giggled some more.

Tiana pulled up her eyebrow while Catherine was looking away, but then got back to the issue at hand.

'You're the star of the party. Don't worry about it. Nobody is going to judge you for what you're wearing. They're all here because they like you.'

Someone in the background whooped, making me want to sink into the ground. I ended the call with a promise to Tiana I would be there soon.

I loved that I had found so many friends over the past year, but being the centre of attention amidst all of them together... It was just too much. I didn't want to be there.

This was the moment I'd known would come. But I'd counted on Thibault to be here and drag me along. Without him here, would I be strong enough to go? I couldn't even decide on what to wear! Maybe I should call Léon and ask him? What time was it in Ann Arbor?

But as much as I missed him and wanted to see his face, I knew he wouldn't care what I wore. I'd talk to him at the end of the day, like I did every day, telling him how much I wished he was here and hearing how much he wished he was here too. Somehow, it never got old. I counted the days until he would return, but right now, it might as well have been a hundred years.

My shoulders sagged, and I turned towards my bed. But then the sight of it stopped me. Was I not a strong woman? Wasn't that what I told myself again and again? Had I not spent too many hours curled up in a bed already? When I left

Franck, I left everything behind that reminded me of him, so this was a different bed. This bed was not meant to be curled up in. This bed was my spread-eagle, strong woman bed!

I dove into the wardrobe and pulled out an unassuming brown dress that I never wore. I was a strong woman, who wasn't going to let anyone rule my life any more. But with this dress, I could at least fade into the background if I wanted. Looking at myself in the mirror, I nodded. That would do. Halfway down the stairs, however, I turned and ran back to grab a bright, coral pink shawl. What if I wanted to be myself after all?

Hiding as much of the stupid brown dress as I could under my pink shawl, I smiled broadly and hugged everyone at my party. This party was a blast! Tiana was amazing. She always knew what I needed.

'*Coucou!* Good to see you.'

'Hi! So glad you could come.'

'I know! Isn't it ridiculous?' This last sentence I uttered to Jeanette Ta, my business partner and soon-to-be manager of the hotel we were set to open in two weeks. I gestured to the massive piñata that Tiana had strung up in the middle of the hall. She'd obviously made it herself, because it was in the shape of an ugly head with crosses for eyes.

Jeanette wrinkled her nose. 'Macabre is the word I'd use. Not particularly fitting?'

'What, you don't recognise him?' Of course she didn't. That head didn't resemble anyone, but I knew the dark hair and moustache were meant to represent those of Franck. Tiana had hung a massive head of Franck at my party, that I was meant to hit with a stick. Leave it to her to come up with that one. Though I appreciated the gesture, I would have preferred not to be reminded of him quite so vividly today.

Jeanette put her fingertips to her lips. 'You don't mean...'

'Hmm.' I took another sip of wine.

While we stood silently staring at the cross-eyed monstrosity, my brother David joined us, also eyeing the piñata. 'Fetching.'

'Thank you.'

'I meant—'

'I know what you meant.'

He sighed, and I took another sip of wine to hide my smirk. He'd got so much better at dealing with my jabs since he took in his 'lodger'. He lived in the family mansion and had donated one of his many spare rooms to a young woman with nowhere else to go. Though he and Maëline were pretty much inseparable, I'd yet to discover the first sign of actual romantic involvement. Leave it to my brother to feel it improper to kiss someone he probably still viewed as his 'charity case'.

'Where's Maëline?'

He stretched his neck to scan the room. 'Around here somewhere. It's not like I'm keeping tabs on her day and night.'

'No?' I teased. 'I think you'd better. If you're not careful, she's going to start having 'appointments'.'

His gaze locked with mine as his eyes narrowed. 'So it's not just me.'

Oh, David. I grinned. 'It's been going on for months.' We'd switched from Maëline to *Maman*. I should have talked to David about it earlier, of course, because as soon as our mother had started mentioning curious appointments without specifying what kind, I'd become suspicious. David, of course, hadn't caught on until months later, and I'd secretly been enjoying watching him work things out. But I was pretty sure I still had some information that would shock him. The anticipation filled me with a childish kind of relish.

His jaw muscles were working overtime. 'You think she's seeing someone?'

Here we go! I felt like jumping up and down with glee, but on the outside I remained calm. 'You think Tiana would have invited him?' With the middle finger of the hand that held my wine glass, I pointed at a large man with a majestic grey beard, who was laughing loudly at something my mother's friend Cédric had said.

David's eyes widened as he produced a strangled noise that would have worried me if I hadn't looked forward to it so much. 'Benoît Le Roux?!' he managed to squeeze out. 'The mayor of Montmales?'

I bit my cheek to keep from howling. This reaction was priceless. 'He's not here for me.'

Panting, David was clutching his glass so hard, I feared the stem would snap. But for someone as proper and stiff as my brother, accepting that his mother might have feelings for a man like Benoît Le Roux must be like trying to fit a wild cat into a matchbox. Benoît was intelligent and kind, but also loud, and he had a certain disregard for the rules, which went against everything David lived by.

I took pity on him and rubbed his arm. 'If it helps, I don't think they're actually together. Yet.' Okay, maybe that was a bit mean, but I couldn't help myself. As long as I lived, I would keep pushing David just that little bit further than he was willing to go. I liked to think it would help him in the rest of his life. Maëline was trying, but she was too sweet, and she was still waiting for him to kiss her. I had no such desires, so it fell to me to prepare my baby brother for a world in which our mother might be dating a man who was nothing like him at all. But even I wouldn't remind him of the fact that our father had not been much of a stickler for rules either.

'Julie! Great party!' Maëline's soft voice barely rose above the hum in the hall. She hugged me while I told her I was glad she was there, but then she noticed my brother's distress. 'David? Is something wrong?'

David needed a few more seconds to regulate his breathing, so I suggested they go and fill up their glasses. When they were sufficiently far away, I called him back. Since he was already out of sorts, I might as well tell him this too. I motioned for him to come closer, and he bent down. Looking him straight in the eye, I said, 'Just kiss her already.'

He staggered back, a wild look in his eyes, and I had to turn to hide my enormous smile. The ability to torture my brother was one of my life's biggest boons.

A woman in her early twenties came skipping my way on pink satin platform heels. The same pink also featured in a skimpy dress that seemed to be made of chiffon handkerchiefs, sewn with one corner onto a kind of silk sack. The thing flowed so much that the woman looked like a cloud. It was actually one of the most elegant garments I'd seen my neighbour in. Anne-Bonny was a social media influencer. She liked my style, and I tried to stay on her good side. You never know when you might need an influencer, right? It usually helped that I had a good-looking male assistant of about her age with me, but today, I'd have to weather her alone.

'I looove the piñata,' Anne-Bonny announced. 'Very avant-garde.'

'Thank you. I have my friend to thank for that.'

'*Je kiffe.* I have to talk to her about this party I'm throwing next month. Maybe she'll have some ideas like that for me.'

'You never know.' I didn't want to disappoint her, but I also didn't want to land Tiana with an overenthusiastic fashionista looking for party ideas. The solution to my problem, however, came from an unexpected side.

'Anne-Bonny, do you know Bella and Isabelle?' I indicated the two women as they approached. Though I was sure they had not been invited, I should have known they'd be here. Bella had been my nemesis since *l'école primaire*, and the butcher's wife always found some way of turning anyone's words into juicy gossip. '*Mes dames*, Anne-Bonny is an influencer. She was just admiring the piñata. I'm sure you both would have plenty more ideas like that for a party, wouldn't you?'

If the shrieks were any indication, these three would hit it off marvellously. I hovered for a minute or so to make it seem like I was genuinely interested in them making a connection, and then I quietly stepped back from the subjects of gold glitter and mother-of-pearl balloons.

As I went to refill my glass, I couldn't help looking around at the people that filled my heart with an intense sense of gratitude. Every person in the hall was here because I was here. If someone would have told me about this moment only a year ago, I would have laughed in their face. Or, more accurately, I probably would have curled up in a corner and cried, not believing it possible. But even though most of the people here knew each other long before I came back to the village, they were here, right now, to show their affection and support for me.

Still, someone was conspicuous by their absence. I glanced at my watch. Ten to three. Beau was probably needlessly flexing his muscles instead of using them to hit that ridiculous head-of-Franck. Then again, Franck was his uncle. Though Thibault had made it clear he hated Franck almost as much as I did, maybe hitting an effigy of his uncle with a stick was a step too far? If he'd known about the thing at all. I frowned at the giant head. My friendship with Beau was the only good thing Franck had ever brought me. But now, the ugly truth came out. Beau wasn't here. Somehow, this was Franck's fault too. I could feel it in my bones.

I strode over to Tiana and interrupted her conversation with my neighbour Auguste Prunille. 'Did you have any particular time in mind?'

She must have seen the bloodlust in my eyes, because she reached behind her and produced a long stick. *'Allez-y.'*

I *would* have a go at him. I'd been dreading this day for four years, but I was a strong woman. Bam! I hit the giant head so hard it swung out of reach. I would not... Bam! ...be ruled... Bam! ...by Franck... Bam! ...any more! Bam! Or Beau. Bam! Or David. Bam! Or... or... men. Bam!

Slightly out of breath, I stopped for a second to admire my handiwork. Though the piñata hadn't burst yet, the damage my hits had done was very satisfying indeed. One of the cross eyes had come off, and the moustache was hanging by a thread. Instead of round, the head was now more of a potato, and a misshapen one at that.

Suddenly, I realised everyone in the room had been cheering me on. My first reaction was to get overheated and embarrassed, but actually... Weren't they on my side? I grinned through my embarrassment and poked the ugly head with my stick. That was all it needed to burst, but instead of sweets, the piñata produced wads of black crepe paper. I stared at the useless pile of crepe, then glanced at Tiana, who shrugged.

'When has Franck ever given you anything good? It felt off to stuff him with goodies. But this...' She pivoted to indicate a curtain behind her that ordinarily hid stacks of chairs when they weren't being used. Lucas now pulled the curtain aside to reveal a table overflowing with beautifully wrapped gifts. '...is what we think of you.'

Tears filled my eyes at the exact moment the church bell chimed three o'clock.

Franck was free.

7

You're not getting involved, are you?

My lower lip wobbled as my eyes searched the crowd for my mother, but her arms came around my shoulders before I spotted her. I held her tightly and cried on her shoulder, not caring that there was an entire hall full of people watching me. If they were there for me, they'd better be there for the bad parts too. And if not, nobody was keeping them here.

But nobody left. Not even Bella and Isabelle. Franck was out of jail. He could do as he pleased. He could come for me and nobody would stop him. But I was in my mother's arms, surrounded by a village full of people who were there for me. And all I could do was cry.

Tiana hugged me from behind. A few seconds later I felt more arms around us, but I squeezed my eyes tightly shut. I couldn't deal with their kindness when I had done nothing to deserve it. But knowing I was not alone – far from it – slowed my breathing back to normal. With one hand I let go of my mother to hold Tiana's hand.

'Thank you,' I whispered.

Both my mother and my best friend softly squeezed me, and I smiled into my mother's shoulder as I let go.

'You're amazing,' I said as I wiped my no doubt puffy, red, mascara-streaked face. 'Both of you. All of you. Thank you,' I added, straightening and addressing the room. I doubted any of them heard my squeaked declaration, but they applauded me nonetheless.

Loud whooping came from my left, where I spotted Marie and her husband Maarten. She wore another one of her princess-worthy outfits, as usual soiled by the hands of her three sons, who had delighted in the array of party food, judging by their dirty, smiling faces.

'You look like you could pass through a little ring,' Marie declared with an appreciative smile. Her penchant for directly translating Dutch expressions often left me flabbergasted, but from her expression, I took it to mean a positive thing, so I smiled my gratitude.

I wished I could let all the people in the room know how much they meant to me, but they'd have to be satisfied with a watery smile as tears welled up again. I hid my face with my hands, and when I dared look again, most people had gone back to talking with each other and enjoying the food and drinks.

'It's okay,' Tiana whispered. 'They know. I think you should leave reading the cards till later, though.'

I gave a weak snort and gently jabbed her in the ribs. It only made her hug me again.

My pink shawl had fallen to the floor at the stroke of three, and I felt as drab as my brown dress. 'Just going to freshen up,' I told Tiana as I recovered my shawl and retreated.

In the ladies, I groaned when I surveyed the damage to my face. Luckily, my contacts were still in place, because I couldn't deal with having to wear both my brown dress *and* my glasses. Even for someone who isn't vain, like me, there are limits.

A voice behind me made me jump. 'Need a hand?'

Maile, my make-up artist, didn't even wait for an answer. She plucked some tissues from her purse and went to work. When she'd finished with my make-up, she pulled a big, sparkly pin from her hair and used it to fasten my shawl to one shoulder. She draped it across my body and tucked it into the belt on my waist. Then she stepped out of her own petticoat and handed it to me.

'How dare you wear that dress to a party,' she scolded, but her tone was more motherly than anything else. It seems all the women in my life were having to take care of me today. Where was that strong woman that wasn't going to let anyone rule her life? Still, with people like Maile, Tiana, and my mother, I couldn't care less if they tried to shepherd me.

As I turned back to the mirror, I almost cried again. Maile's magic had done it again. The petticoat spread out my skirt, together with the shawl transforming my ugly dress into a lively party ensemble.

'Don't you start.' Maile wiggled her finger at me. 'You know that mascara isn't waterproof.' She hooked her arm through mine. 'Now, let's go find a glass with a stem.'

Feeling much more confident now that I looked the part, I took in the view of the hall and all the people in it. Tiana really had invited pretty much the entire village. Underneath the *vendanges* painting, my neighbour Auguste and his neighbour and former enemy Gilles de Vigan were laughing and drinking together. After my discovery about Gilles's past, the two older men had miraculously managed to patch things up and had been firm friends ever since. They raised their glass to me, and I inclined my head with a wide smile. Maybe, in some cases, I *had* done some good for the village.

Underneath the sorry remains of the piñata, Anne-Bonny was hard at work creating content for her social media accounts. She threw the wads of black paper up in the air, letting them rain down on her like autumn leaves while she posed for her phone camera, set up on a little tripod nearby. I'd already seen her wink at it over a glass of *crémant*. Straight at it, in profile, and over her shoulder.

Since she'd moved in next door, I'd started following her accounts and sometimes left a comment on one of her photos. With the thousands of followers she had, I doubted she ever saw them, but the quality of her pictures had improved over time. They were still overexposed to my eyes, but apparently, that was her style.

David had joined the little group of party-goers that contained *Maman* and Benoît Le Roux. He kept glancing at the jolly man, obviously trying to join in the cheer, but it looked painful. I rolled my lips between my teeth to keep from grinning, but it didn't work.

'Not so bad after all, *hein*?' Tiana bumped my shoulder with hers.

'They're a great bunch of people,' I said, beaming.

'Hey, where's Beau? I haven't seen your man candy yet.'

It was a good thing I'd been so happy just a moment before, because coming down from a lower high would have put me into negative territory. Why wasn't he here? 'You mean boy candy. But I suppose he is eye candy,' I had to admit. 'He had a thing.'

Tiana tucked in her chin and raised an eyebrow at me. 'A thing? Now?'

I shrugged.

She blinked a few times, then stood next to me, silently staring at our friends having fun. 'Well, we all deal with bad news in different ways. Maybe his way is to be alone.'

He's not alone. The words were on the tip of my tongue, but why complicate things? 'Maybe.'

'Ooh, this'll cheer you up. Do you know who's coming to the Gala Lumières?'

Lyon's big film festival was only on the periphery of my interests, so I did not.

'Captain Canon, The Defier, *and* T-Roar!'

I made a face. 'Who?'

She flapped her hands like a child. 'Oh, come on. Even you must have seen some of the trailers. The superheroes? I mean, the actors, of course. Simon Dell, Ben Hjerson, and Ken Doo are coming *here*. Lucas and I have already got tickets for all the events. You have *got* to join us for at least one of them.'

How to get out of this politely? As my best friend, Tiana should have known superhero movies weren't my thing. The frizzy curls of Madame Dufaux appeared in our vision. She seemed agitated. 'I'm sorry I'm late. My husband made lunch, which was very good because he's a marvellous cook. But he clears his workspace into my workspace, the sink. How does he expect me to clean things if I can't even reach the tap?'

Tiana smirked, blessedly forgetting about the superheroes. 'You don't fool me, you know. Everyone knows you and Monsieur Vray have the best relationship in the Département du Rhône.'

Blushing, Madame Dufaux glanced at Lucas. 'I think you'll find you have to have *something* to bemoan about your husband. If they were perfect, you'd start to doubt yourself!'

This made Tiana laugh, and Madame Dufaux relaxed a little. 'Anyway, so I was late already, and then I got into this whole commotion at the church.'

Tiana and I looked at each other. 'What commotion?' I asked.

'I'm not sure.' She tapped her lip. 'Lots of police and people in those white suits you see on TV, *tu sais*?'

Tiana's eyebrows came together in a frown. 'Police? At the church?'

Madame Dufaux had spotted the snacks and was already on her way, but I wrinkled my nose at my friend. 'I've had enough police for one day. Someone died at the Centre de Prédiction earlier, just before we got there on our walk.'

'Oh, how awful.' Then her expression changed from sympathy to suspicion. 'You're not getting involved, are you?'

I huffed. 'Why on earth would I do that? The only death I want to see is...' I stopped. I'd been about to say Franck's, but was that true? There had absolutely been times when I wished him dead. But even knowing he'd been released not an hour ago and he might well be out for revenge, I didn't wish him ill any longer. All I wanted was for him to leave me alone. No, not alone. With a village full of friends.

Tiana put an arm around me and steered me towards the table of snacks. 'Have you tried this ham and olive cake? It's amazing, just saying.'

'It's yours, isn't it.' That wasn't even a question. Tiana didn't really bake. She made one thing, and one thing only. This savoury cake. Granted, it was always good, so I took a slice.

The party went on for another hour before people started to leave. Tiana sent me home with my family, forbidding me to help clean up. She had enough help, she said, and true enough, there were already several people going round with bin bags. Céline gave me a little wave.

David grabbed both my shoulders and pushed me out the door. He, Maëline, and my mother were keeping me company for a while. To show me photos from their trip, David had lied. I was sure there'd be pictures, but I knew it was mostly to prevent me from feeling alone after the party. No doubt that had been my mother's idea, or it might have been Maëline's. David might not even realise that was the true purpose of his visit. Then again, sometimes he surprised me. He was certainly displaying his human side, telling stories about what Maëline and he had been up to in Canada while we walked the short distance to my house.

Their second holiday together. I cast some covert glances at Maëline, but she was simply enjoying his tales and her own memories. As I opened my door to them and hung my coat, I wondered if I'd been wrong all along. Maybe they really were just friends. In that case, I'd well and truly put my foot in it, telling him to kiss her. Ay...

'What a wonderful party,' Maëline said as she poured herself a glass of water. 'Tiana knows what she's doing. Does she have a background in event planning?'

That was so far from Tiana's character that I snort-laughed. 'No! She hates crowds. But to us, this wasn't a crowd. These were just our friends, the people we grew up with. It's easy to have fun with the people you like.'

She gave me a warm smile, but then bit her lip, narrowing her eyes. 'I still don't understand the piñata, though. David told me it was supposed to be your ex-husband, but was he really that bad? None of you ever mention him.'

We'd moved to the living room, where both David and my mother suddenly discovered all kinds of spots on the ceiling and walls that needed their immediate attention, so I found my courage and explained. 'He's a criminal. They released him today, after he spent four years in jail for fraud. Fraud against me and my clients.'

Maëline's hand went to her neck. 'What? Why would he defraud his own wife?'

'Oh, no, this was after I left him. He... treated me badly, so I left him. At the time, all I had was a beauty blog that I expanded in order to make a little money. It actually did quite well, which further wounded Franck's ego. But I only found out he was a cybercriminal after he hacked my business and destroyed it, leaving most of my clients with no money and no products, and me with no money and no reputation. But because I had nothing to lose, I testified against him. I've had four years to build my life back up, but from today, I'll have to start looking over my shoulder again.'

'No, you don't,' my mother exclaimed with such vehemence that it startled me. 'You don't have to look over your shoulder if you have friends and family to watch your back.'

My wonderful mother. I swallowed but could only squeeze her hand if I didn't want to ruin Maile's handiwork.

'A beauty blog? How interesting. What did you sell, make-up?' Maëline's unsubtle attempt at changing the subject chased away the lump in my throat.

'Yes, but also skin and hair care products. I studied to be an aesthetician,' I added with a half smile. What life had that been in? *Maman* had wanted me to go to university, but instead, I went with Franck. Finding life away from the village rather lonely, I'd enrolled in a few courses after all. This was, of course, before Franck started shutting me off from the world one person at a time.

Maëline started peppering me with questions about skin care and make-up, seamlessly weaving it into a story about a woman's make-up she'd seen in Canada, which led us to go through the other holiday snaps, and before I knew it, the clock chimed seven and the door to the kitchen opened. I perked up, expecting to see Thibault, but instead, Jacqueline entered the living room.

'Hi all. Sorry I couldn't make it to the party.' She sagged down on the couch next to me. 'What a day. It was supposed to be my day off!' Her head fell back on the cushion as we all patiently waited for more ranting. But I should have known, that was not Jacqueline's style. She turned her head towards me. 'Did you have a good time? Oh! Thank Tiana for me. She brought some of her ham and olive cake over to the church, and I was so hungry that I scarfed it down and forgot to thank her.'

'You were at the church too? Weren't you busy already?'

She scrubbed her face with her hands. 'Did you not hear me say "What a day"? Three deaths, all on the same day. My day off.'

'Who else died?' I asked. 'And I'm guessing, if you were involved, the others weren't natural deaths either?'

A quick thinning of her lips was the only sign that showed Jacqueline's humanity. Being a police officer, she was used to seeing more misery than most of us, but three unnatural deaths was a lot, even for her. 'A local artist was copying one of the church's paintings when they were attacked.'

'Who would murder someone in a church?' Maëline clasped her hands in her lap, which David carefully covered with his.

'Probably someone with a grudge or two. They used a paint-brush.'

I tried to picture it, but couldn't. 'How?'

Jacqueline pointed at her eye and we all winced. 'Didn't your mother tell you?'

I glanced at *Maman*. Of course, as mayor, she would have known about this.

My mother straightened her skirt, making sure there wasn't a crease to be seen. 'None of her business. She's been involved with enough murders, I think.'

Jacqueline grinned. 'Right you are. We don't want her to get involved. Remember the last one? Can't win 'em all, *mon amie*.'

'Sound advice,' David agreed. 'But you said three deaths? Who's the last one?'

'A gallery owner in Villefranche. But my colleague is deal-ing with that one. He may be an idiot, but it looks like an open-and-shut case. You didn't hear that. He's a good cop. He'll have it solved in no time. No reason to get involved.'

I held up my hands with a smile, though I couldn't help feeling a little sour about their dismissal. I had solved the last case, even if I hadn't made my findings public. 'Don't worry. There's absolutely no way I'm getting dragged into this one. Any of them. I promise.'

8

Come over to my studio so I can show you

Thinking Thibault would probably be back any minute, I could let my family leave after a light supper of beetroot and dandelion salad with nuts and grilled goat cheese, giving them an honest promise that I would be fine. Tiana had dropped off all my presents, and I was looking forward to unwrapping them and marvelling at the generosity of my friends.

I nestled myself on the couch with a big mug of *tisane* and took a random package from the pile in front of me. It was a round box about the size of a small watermelon or a large cantaloupe, wrapped in sparkly paper with a big pink bow. It was the girliest present of the lot, and I had to open that one first. It contained a gorgeous, silvery fascinator. Unlike many of the kind, it wasn't flashy with lots of feathers and bows, but almost understated, with puffs of very fine gauze dappled with tiny rhinestones. One silver flower pulled the eye in and didn't let go. I didn't have to look at the card to know this was from Marie.

I twirled the fascinator in my hands, admiring its simple elegance. I even put it on my head and took a selfie that I sent to my friend with too many heart emojis. With some difficulty, I managed to put the pretty thing back in its box to move on to the next present. Which to choose?

My hands went to a big, rectangular box wrapped in simple, moss green paper. *From Gilles*, the card read. Interesting. Though I'd known Gilles all my life, we didn't know each other all that well. He owned the wine bar in the village and he liked modern art, but would this gift have anything to do with either of those facts? I ripped the paper to reveal a sturdy cardboard box. Inside the box was a painting. My first thought was 'yuck'. It wasn't abstract, as Gilles preferred his art, because I recognised the landscape. It was my house. I knew exactly where the artist had stood to paint it, but instead of the rolling, organic shapes that I loved so much, the artist had focussed on the angles. My house and garden looked hard and forbidding.

I sighed. Despite my dislike of its style, the fact that Gilles had gone through the trouble of finding this painting, or maybe even commissioning it, made me weepy. Actually, I liked the way the sun struck my white currant bush there. And was that Henri, the stray cat that lived in my garden? I peered at the little grey blob and decided it was Henri, whether the artist had intended it to be or not. I now had a painting of Henri!

I sent a text to Gilles, thanking him for his thoughtful gift and then, on a whim, googled the artist. Good thing Google corrected me, because I'd read the name as Régis Piquemal, but it turned out to be Piguemal, a name I'd never heard before. Silly me. The internet shouted at my ignorance of this super famous artist whose work had sky-rocketed in price after his mysterious death.

Not more death… I threw my phone to the side and continued unwrapping my goodies. An hour and a mountain of wrapping paper later, my mascara was on a pile of tissues again, but I was feeling thoroughly blessed and equally exhausted.

'How was the party, *chérie*?' Léon asked after I answered his call on my watch. I was already in bed, keeping myself up to be able to talk to him. Since he was six hours behind, my evenings were the middle of the day for him, so he made the call when he had time.

'Amazing. It would have been better with you there, but I'm so blown away by people's kindness. Tomorrow, I'll show you all my presents. How are you?'

My eyes were drooping, and Léon gave a soft chuckle. 'I have nothing new to say. I've been thinking of you.'

'Hmm.' I smiled, my eyes closing in the process.

'Good night, darling.'

'Hi Jessica, it's Julie Belmain.' Feeling ridiculous. Why was I calling her? I wasn't Thibault's mother. I had no right or reason to worry about him if he didn't come home for the night. Two nights, but I wasn't keeping an eye on him, really. I only had a first appointment scheduled for today as well, so I didn't need him here. But...

'Hi?' None of the judgement I felt in my head was actually in her tone, but she was clearly wondering why I called.

'I'm looking for Thibault. He wasn't here this morning, and... well...' Ugh, I sounded like a possessive ex-girlfriend. 'I'm sorry, I shouldn't have called. It's none of my business.'

Jessica chuckled. 'Don't worry, you're not intruding. Unfortunately though, I can't tell you where he is. He left shortly after the police arrived, and I haven't heard from him since.'

My breath caught. 'The police? For him?'

'No, no. For me. Well, not for me. Yet. I mean...' She gave a frustrated sigh. 'My ex was murdered and they think I did it.'

Uh oh.

'Oh, hey!'

Don't say it.

'Didn't you solve a murder a few months ago?'

'Err...'

'You think you could help me out if I tell you my side of the story?'

No. 'I'm afraid it's not that easy. My friend with the police told me her colleague is a good cop who will solve the case in no time.' Technically, she did say that. 'I think you can trust him to find out the truth.'

'Hm. That's what Alain said.'

Who was Alain? 'Smart man.'

'You think so? He seems to be. Do you know him?'

How should I know? I knew an Alain. Maybe it was him. I didn't have to answer, as Jessica had moved on.

'I'd really like to talk to someone who's dealt with all this before, though... Is there any chance you'd have time today?'

Was there? Sure, I had time. And I felt bad for Jessica that she was in this situation. But did I really want to get involved with yet another murder? Then again, I wasn't really involved if all I did was listen to someone talk. 'Of course. After lunch?'

'Yes.' She sounded relieved, which strengthened my belief that I was doing the right thing. 'Come over to my studio so I can show you.'

Show me what? 'All right, see you then.'

I hung up and stared at my phone. I'd only spoken with Jessica Rose a handful of times. I liked her, but she had a way of assuming everyone could look inside her head, or smell what she meant by something she said.

With a shake of my head, I returned to my earlier worry: I still didn't know where Beau was. But more importantly, was he still angry at me? Was that why he'd stayed away? But he hadn't come home the night before either, and we hadn't fought then. Was it even to do with me? But in that case, why didn't he just talk to me instead of taking it out on me?

I blew out a breath. A lot of 'me' in that chain of thought. Perhaps I was making myself too important in the problem Thibault obviously had. Instead, I decided to focus on my ten o'clock appointment. Maile would be there too, because my client wanted to be sure my make-up artist could handle dark skin. My assurances that Maile had dealt with every kind of skin tone before had resulted in a rather special-snowflakey raised eyebrow. This client was used to hearing 'yes'.

I dug up my most humble attitude – had to dig quite deep for it – and went to greet Maile. Ten minutes and counting.

An hour and a half later, I felt like fanning myself.

'And that's why Gío gave Beau the Duo-Glide.'

I leaned back, astonished after Maile's story. She'd lingered after my client had left. We'd needed a shot of caffeine after bowing to the Queen of Pernickety. I'd moaned about the fact that Beau would have made the appointment a whole lot easier and wondered aloud if he'd become indispensable to my business, and somehow, this had led Maile to recount her life's story. Now I wondered why I'd never heard it before. Or maybe not. It wasn't a story you told a stranger at a bus stop. But after three years of working together, I must have reached Maile's circle of intimates.

That, I could believe. I still had trouble, however, seeing Thibault in the heroic role Maile had cast him in. But it did explain how a young man who'd, according to his own words, escaped his criminal family, could have afforded a vintage Harley. Up till now, I'd chosen not to think about it, hoping he'd found it, or come by it in some other not entirely illegal way. Instead, it had been a gift. For saving his friends' lives. Huh.

I stared at the cast-iron spiral staircase leading to Thibault's lair. He'd never said anything about this. It seemed to me that he'd be shouting it from the rooftops if he'd helped bring down an international crime organisation. Had Maile made the whole thing up, just now? Her story of bravery in the face of death did not correspond to the awkward man-boy I knew. I turned to study her, but she hid her face behind her mug. Was that an amused twinkle in her eye? I felt like I'd been had, but if she'd spun me a yarn, then how *did* Beau end up with such an expensive motorcycle?

The question kept my mind reeling all the way through a lunch of leftovers and my drive to Jessica Rose's studio. Ordinarily, I liked to honour tradition and keep a little *sieste* after lunch to let the food settle and boost alertness afterwards, but I'd had a relatively light meal and I'd rather get this talk with Jessica over with. It couldn't be as shocking as the story I'd just heard, though. The more I thought about it, the less I believed Maile's extraordinary tale. By the time I pulled up to the ugly, concrete building that housed Jessica's studio, I was shaking my head at myself for ever having given credit to Maile's words. She was a better liar than I'd thought. The way she'd told the story, it seemed perfectly plausible that her father was some kind of scientist spy, but now, I wanted to look up what movie she'd retold with herself in the starring role.

As soon as I opened my car door, though, a shrill voice drove all further thought of the ridiculous story from my mind. I couldn't hear what was being shouted, but I didn't think the voice was Jessica's, so I hurried inside to come to her aid.

The tiny kitchen seemed full to bursting with two women gesticulating wildly at each other around a tall man in the middle who was trying to calm them down.

'You keep out of this,' a greying blonde woman with a pony-tail shrieked at the man.

His low voice did nothing to calm her down. 'If you stop accusing J—'

'Accusing?' she yelled. 'Is it accusing when I'm mad at her for *not* doing anything?'

9

I didn't do it!

Jessica glared at Anaëlle Sandhomme. 'What, you would have preferred it if I *had* killed him?'

'Yes!'

Though she knew Anaëlle from before she came to the Beaujolais, Jessica still found her difficult to deal with. And her timing was the absolute worst.

After the police had left the day before, Alain had stayed.

'Didn't you want to go with them?' Jessica had asked him.

He'd shrugged. 'Like I told them, I don't think you murdered anyone. I thought that maybe you wouldn't want to be alone after receiving that kind of news. But if you do, I can call a taxi?'

She'd let him stay. She'd even told him all about her history with Xavier Grosse. Then he'd asked about her art, and before she knew it, it was ten o'clock at night.

'As much as I'm enjoying your enthusiasm,' Alain had said, 'I'd better call that taxi if I want to have any chance of finding a hotel for the night. Would you mind if I come back tomorrow to have another look at the space before I try to find out who owns it now?'

As usual, her mouth had run away from her brain. 'If you're going to come back anyway, you might as well sleep on the couch.'

His surprised laugh had made her blush from her hair down to her toes. 'You've just told me how much you make from these statues. You must be a very trusting person if you don't expect me to load them into your car and take off during the night.'

She'd glanced at her spiky blobs, then at the floor, before settling her gaze on her fingernails.

'I would like to stay. If you're sure,' he'd said.

She'd let out a silly little giggle. When was she ever sure about the things she said? 'I'll get you a blanket.'

She'd returned with a blanket and the bottle of wine Anaëlle had given her for her birthday nine months ago. She sat on the couch next to him. 'One condition. Tell me about you. I know you've done some construction work and you now want to start your own company from here, but I want to know about you.'

He'd readily agreed and told her about his family and growing up in Vienne, south of Lyon. He liked winter sports and sailing the Mediterranean but hated boasters. When the bottle was empty, she felt she knew him well enough to trust him. Or at least to trust him enough to let him stay. Whether it was the wine or her own sense telling her that, she didn't care. What else was she going to do at that hour?

Not being used to alcohol, she'd retreated to the office space where she'd made her bedroom after telling him where he could find clean towels. It hadn't taken long for her to fall into a deep sleep until the smell of coffee had woken her.

When she stumbled into the kitchen, Alain had already taken her broom into the showroom space, so she went through her morning routine and had her hands full of clay by the time she first saw him. He must have been optimistic about renting the space from whoever owned it now, because he'd spent hours cleaning and rearranging everything that wasn't nailed down. All morning they'd smiled at each other whenever they met, but both had been engrossed in their work – he was on the phone when she brought him a coffee and she'd been concentrating on her sculpting when he poked his head into the studio. So by lunchtime, she'd been desperate for some actual interaction, preferably of the intimate kind they'd shared the night before. All they'd done was talk, but she had high hopes for today.

Alain had come into the kitchen when she was drying her hands, getting ready to make lunch. 'Thanks again for letting me stay,' he'd said, leaning against the kitchen counter. 'Apparently, there's some mix-up with the will and it won't be read until tomorrow, so nobody knows who owns the building now. I think it's perfect for my purposes, so provided I can convince the next owner to rent it out to me, you'll be seeing quite a lot of me in the future.'

Jessica had produced a spuriously shy smile. 'You say that as if I'd mind.'

He sidled along the counter. Jessica dropped the towel. 'I was hoping you wouldn't.' He was close enough now that Jessica could feel his warmth. 'I've been wanting to kiss you ever since you almost ran me over.'

All she could do was lift her chin, and he took the hint, but before their lips met, the kitchen door opened.

'I've brought *déjeuner*. Who are you?'

So, timing. Not Anaëlle's strong suit. They'd divided the Vietnamese food over the two plates and one of the food boxes Anaëlle brought, and it had taken all of lunch to get Anaëlle to warm to at least the idea of a man being present in her friend's studio, if not to the man himself.

But as soon as Anaëlle calmed down about Alain, she'd remembered the original purpose of her visit – to discuss the murder of Xavier. Which, it turned out, she believed Jessica had committed.

As much as Jessica had at first doubted her decision to let Alain stay, right now she was happy to have a literal buffer between herself and her stubborn friend. How could she not believe in Jessica's innocence?

The sound of someone clearing their throat alerted them all to the person standing in the doorway.

'Julie!' Jessica rushed towards the newcomer. 'Julie, I'm so glad you're here. Have you heard from Thibault yet?'

Not that she cared too much about Thibault right now, but since he was the topic of Julie's phone call that morning, it seemed only polite to ask. When Julie shook her head, though, a slight pang of guilt slithered through Jessica's stomach. She couldn't imagine Beau was in any kind of trouble, but Julie was clearly worried about him. Still, Jessica's own worries were undoubtedly more substantial. She'd practically been accused of murder!

They moved from the kitchen to Jessica's studio. With the arrival of another woman, Anaëlle had finally calmed down, and Jessica led them all to the sitting area. She sagged down on one of the beanbags, massaging her temples while she rested her head on the soft cover. Alain shoved the blanket he'd used last night to the side and he and Julie took a seat on the couch. Anaëlle was still too agitated to sit, so she paced a bit and tapped her foot in a seriously annoying manner.

'Will you stop?' Jessica snapped at her. 'This has nothing to do with you.'

'He sold my art too, you know.' Anaëlle crossed her arms but thankfully stopped pacing and tapping, bringing Jessica to swallow the nasty remark about both the quality and the quantity of her friend's art that she had been about to spew. Anaëlle didn't deserve that, anyway. Her art, mostly paintings of broken things with jagged edges, might only cater to a niche market, but within that market she was highly regarded.

Jessica became aware of an awkward silence and hastened to introduce her guests to each other. 'Julie, this is Alain Coquard. He's staying here for... a bit. And this is my friend Anaëlle Sandhomme. She's also an artist. This is Julie Belmain. She's kind of the local unofficial murder solver.'

Julie vigorously shook her head. 'I'm really not. We have the police for that.'

Jessica huffed. With the arrival of Anaëlle, a headache had begun to build that was now reaching legendary proportions. 'Yeah, I've seen the police in action. That policeman thinks I did it. Just because it was my artwork that... Not even mine! One of *his*!' She held her hands up as if offering the entire mess to the photographer on her couch.

Julie narrowed her eyes and bit her lip. 'If you want me to understand any of this, you'll have to give me more than that. Start at the beginning. This is about... your ex, you said? Tell me more about him. What was he like?'

'He was a fraudulent pig,' Jessica spat.

'She should have killed him much earlier,' Anaëlle threw in.

'I didn't kill him!' Jessica hit the side of the beanbag as she whipped her head round to her friend.

'If I may?' Alain raised both eyebrows at Jessica, then turned to Julie at Jessica's weary nod. 'I only met Jessica yesterday when she kindly let me stay here. After the police came to tell her about the death of Xavier Grosse—'

'He'd been an X all his life. You should have known,' Anaëlle grumbled, but a glare from Jessica silenced her.

'We went through the whole story together,' Alain resumed.

Julie frowned. 'I can imagine. Why would you stay with someone you don't know who's just been accused of murder?'

This was off to a great start. Julie didn't seem to trust Alain either. Anaëlle's reaction was predictable, but if Julie didn't like him, maybe there was something off with Jessica's judgement of character? She had dated Xavier, after all.

'They didn't actually accuse her. And...' One corner of his mouth ticked up and made Jessica's stomach jump. 'Let's just say I didn't feel threatened.'

Smooth. Was he calling her weak? She glanced at Anaëlle, who glowered at him. But then, she'd been doing that since she arrived. Her distrust of men was legendary. How Xav had ever talked her into letting him sell her stuff... Just showed how good he was at what he did. Or, used to do. She still couldn't quite believe he was really gone.

Alain continued, 'Jessica met Xavier through Anaëlle.'

Jessica bobbed her head left and right, which felt odd, lying on the beanbag. 'Xavier was the dealer for several people in the Village, so I heard about him there, but Anaëlle introduced us.'

Alain started to explain, 'The Village being—'

'The artists' commune in Jarnioux,' Julie finished with a nod.

'Right. You're obviously from around here. I'm not. Neither was Jessica, but she knew about the Village from friends, so that's where she went when she left Marseille. When she and Xavier got together, he offered her the use of this place, but by then he'd already sold several of Jessica's classical pieces.'

Jessica squeezed her eyes shut. How taken he'd been with her torsos. He'd praised her skill and the originality of painting them with different skin tones, including freckles, moles, scars, and one with vitiligo. That was, until he discovered she made other kinds of sculptures too.

'But in the end, her abstract pieces took off and made her famous,' Alain said.

'And him a shedload of money,' Anaëlle interjected.

Julie got up and bent over one of several spiky and menacing-looking blobby sculptures. 'You mean these?'

'Yah, I know.' Jessica groaned. Then she jumped up and joined Julie in front of her sculptures. It was nice of Alain to try and make a sensible story out of her bits and pieces of information, but this was her work, her passion. She needed to explain it in order for Julie to fully understand the weight of the situation. 'Look, I studied long and hard to make this stuff' – she waved her hand at the collection of half-formed torsos that littered the space – 'but sometimes I just want to let loose on a chunk of clay. It's pure abstract expression, which, to me, doesn't even mean much. It's a palate cleanser. Like a literary author keeping a diary – rage on the page. It doesn't require any particular skill, but that's the stuff that people wanted. They valued it for exactly that: the feeling in it.'

She pushed one spiky blob with the tip of her finger, making it wobble. 'It's like when a classical painter gets famous for his five-minute cartoons. I'm not knocking it, because these no-brainer pieces pay for my studio, and they are still *my* art.'

Julie nodded sympathetically, and Jessica rushed on.

'But Xavier made it happen. He made it valuable. His job, and his talent, was talking – making waves, building anticipation and excitement... Basically making up stuff about the art he was selling that resonated with his buyers, whether it actually had something to do with what the artist intended or not. He knew the right people. The people who know how to turn a work of art into a profit by playing the market: driving up prices, trading with insider knowledge, overvaluing a piece they then donate to get a bigger tax write-off – only super-rich people, of course. Us mere mortals can hardly get into the building. Even I, as the artist, am only allowed to attend certain functions. And then there's the outright illegal aspects...'

She had to stop. During her explanation, she'd felt her jaw muscles clench, and the last words had come out through gritted teeth. Trudging back to the beanbag, she tried to force herself to relax.

'If you knew he was breaking the law, why didn't you go to the police?' Julie asked. She'd taken her place on the couch again, so Jessica plopped down on the beanbag.

'I didn't know. Not at first. But I found out fairly quickly that he'd tricked me too. He'd kind of talked me into liking him, if that makes sense. He was really good at making you see a golden future with whatever it was he was selling you. In my case, that was him. Reality turned out to be less golden. But I was afraid that he'd kick me out of my studio if I ended things with him. Of course, by the time I just couldn't deal with his ego any more, I was ready to give up my space. But I should have known he'd let me keep it. Still made him money, didn't I? He made sure to convince me he was still the right person to bring my art to the people, even if he wasn't the right person for me.'

Her fingers played with the fabric of her skirt while she stared at a spot on the couch between Julie and Alain. 'So we kept our relationship professional for a while. Until two days ago.' She fisted the fabric and stamped her foot on the floor, which didn't make as much of a sound as she'd hoped, since she couldn't put much force on it from her position on the bean-bag. Pressing her eyes closed, Jessica jerked her head to the side. Someone else could take it from here.

'Captain Chrome cheated her,' she heard Anaëlle say after a few seconds. Relieved that her friend would finally stick up for her, Jessica relaxed her hands and shot Anaëlle a grateful look. Julie had her hands palms upwards on her knees, lingering there from the last unspoken question. She now spread her fingers again at Anaëlle's confusing statement.

Anaëlle rubbed her index finger over the base of the fingers on her other hand. 'Big silver rings. Showed everyone how cool he thought he was. But he sold fakes of Jessica's work.'

'AI!' Jessica burst out. 'He didn't just make fakes. He fed my work into a machine and had it print out more of the same. And his clients couldn't even tell the difference!' She threw her head back on the beanbag. That had perhaps stung even more than his betrayal. It wasn't the emotion she'd put into her work after all. It was simply the tale he'd told them that they bought. Just like she had.

'He took all the life and soul out of it. A machine can't express itself! Yes, those pieces are just as random as mine, but when I make them, they represent what I feel at that moment. People buy my pieces for the emotion. If you take that away, what are they paying for? I know the end result is the same, but it's the fact that he used my name to sell them that I object to. If he had taken my art and had that machine produce similar pieces, he might have got away with it, but when he used my name, that's when it became forgery. Those pieces became fakes. Worthless.'

Unable to feel anything any more after all the emotion she'd dealt with in the last two days, Jessica stared at the ceiling. When Julie asked how she'd found out, the words barely reached her consciousness, but she heard Alain answer.

'She was looking on Xavier's website to see if he still had her torsos up for sale when she saw a statue listed as one of hers that she didn't recognise. She called Xavier to ask him about it, but he was evasive and told her to come over in the morning when he was in his office. That's when he told her what he'd done. He wasn't sorry for it either. Said he'd make sure she was paid for her original input, but the pieces weren't worthless if people were still willing to pay for them.'

Art is worth whatever people are willing to pay for it. Jessica could still hear Xavier say it. He'd always said it, ever since she met him. But back then he was talking about her abstract pieces in relation to her torsos. She'd thought him quite sensible then. What an idiot she'd been.

'She told him what she thought of him and left.'

Jessica almost laughed. Had Alain not heard her scream when he came through town? She thought all of Villefranche must have heard her shriek in Xavier's face. She *had* told him exactly what she thought of him. But she hadn't been all that civil about it. And she absolutely would have physically attacked him, too, especially when he tried to get rid of her because he had 'another appointment', if she hadn't felt faint and realised she hadn't eaten yet. Strange, how your body can help you out like that sometimes, without you even knowing.

'Then around lunchtime, the police came here to tell us Xavier had been murdered,' Alain concluded.

'Small wonder,' Anaëlle muttered.

Her constant negativity irked Jessica. 'You're losing money here, too, you know?'

'Exactly. So I have no motive.'

'Oh, and I do have motive, therefore, I am the killer?'

'He *was* stabbed – *in the back* – with one of *your* works. Or a fake one, which makes it even more poignant.' Anaëlle held her hands up in defence when Jessica gasped. 'I'm only saying, if you did do it, I'm behind you. *C'est normale.*'

'But I didn't do it!'

'All right, all right.' She clearly still didn't believe Jessica.

'I saw him drive off, so he was alive at ten. And the other-appointment person talked to him after I left.'

'Only, the police say there was no other appointment in his diary,' Alain said, more to Julie than to Jessica.

'And that's more or less why I wanted to talk to you about this.' Jessica held her hand out to Julie. 'Xavier was so meticulous. Everything got written down. It makes no sense that he'd tell me he had another appointment – and I know he did, because I heard him talking to a woman after I left – but he wouldn't have that appointment in his calendar.'

Julie narrowed her eyes. 'So... you talked to Xavier...'

Jessica nodded.

'Then you left to get some food or something?'

Another nod.

'What time was this?'

'I went to see him as soon as his gallery opened, at nine, and I left at something like twenty to ten.'

'Then how did you see him drive off at ten?'

'Well, I wasn't done with him.' *Obviously?* 'I was just going to get something to eat and then shout at him some more. I didn't care whether this other person would still be there or not. They deserved to hear the truth about him too. But when I came back with renewed energy, his ridiculous black SUV pulled out of the parking lot behind the building. He held his hand up to me, rings flashing and everything, and he just drove off. But the police don't believe me.'

Julie pursed her lips. 'Did he tell you anything about the person he was going to see next?'

Jessica shook her head. 'Nothing. I only know it was a woman because I heard her voice.'

'You didn't see her come in?'

'I left via the fire escape round the back. That leads to the parking lot, which also leads to the shops on the street running parallel to the one the gallery's on. I told the police to ask the guy in the sandwich shop to vouch for me, but they said I could have gone into the shop after I killed Xavier and made up the part about seeing him drive off.'

'Any idea where he might have gone?'

Jessica shrugged. 'Again, nothing in his diary.'

'So you need to find the woman.'

Both Jessica and Alain nodded. Anaëlle studied her fingernails, which led Julie to narrow her eyes and direct a question at her. 'Do you have any idea who this woman might have been?'

Anaëlle jumped visibly. 'Me? No! Why would I know anything about this?'

10

There is no case

Suspicious. If I had taken anything away from my visit to Jessica's, it was that her friend, that Anaëlle, was suspicious. As was that man, by the way, who just happened to meet her when she was about to be caught up in a murder investigation and still wanted to stay. Sus. Pish. Us.

But! It had nothing to do with me. I had promised Jacqueline I'd stay out of murder investigations, and I intended to do as I'd said. That's what I'd told Jessica as well, so though I'd offered help with anything else she might need, my hands were clean.

If only my mind were as clean. I wasn't going to do any digging, but I couldn't help thinking about all three of these murders. So close together, in both time and space – were they really separate? A personal assistant, a painter, and a gallery owner. At least two of them had the artistic connection. I wondered if the painter had lived in the artists' commune in Jarnioux as well. And whether Jessica's ex had been his dealer. But the police would find that out soon enough. If they knew each other, the murders almost had to be connected, so perhaps that would make them easier to solve.

Chloé Walkure's secretary, though… But then, she might not have been murdered. I had assumed so because Chloé had said her assistant was happy and had no reason to take her own life. But Jacqueline had only said 'death', not 'murder'.

I had just reached home and draped my coat over a kitchen chair, when the front door opened again, and my mother's voice called out, *'Coucou!'*

'In here,' I answered.

She entered the kitchen with a sigh. 'What a way to spend your day off.'

I waited patiently for the explanation to that while I searched for Xavier Grosse on my phone. The first hit was a news item about his death, but the second was an image taken from the gallery website. An amiable-looking black man smiled into the camera, making me sad that such a lovely smile would no longer brighten the world before I remembered Jessica's accusations about him.

'I've spent the entire morning trying to console Chloé. I haven't even had lunch! She just cannot believe Wylène would kill herself. Especially in such an unpleasant manner.'

Getting up to reheat the last bit of lunch that I'd saved for Beau in doubtful optimism, I asked, 'So what did happen?'

Maman sighed again. 'Yesterday, after you left, I spent most of the time with her just hearing about how wonderful the girl had been, how she'd been the rock that Chloé had built her empire on... You know, all the good things people remember first. By the time I left to come to your party, she was sad, but no longer in shock. I didn't ask for details then, because I didn't want to upset her and frankly, because I wanted to focus on you. But she had me promise to return today, which I did.'

So far, so normal. I put the plate of mushroom pasta in front of my mother in the hope that she would get to the point and deliver some actual information. But she first took a bite, making an appreciative and grateful noise. Then another, and another, before she finally swallowed and said, 'Diet pills.'

Excuse me? There wasn't that much butter and cream in my dish.

'The illegal kind. The kind that burn up your insides. Chloé pulled some heavy strings and had the police prioritise Wylène's case. They found *grattons* in her stomach, along with a fatal dose of DNP, which Chloé told me is some kind of fat-burning drug that also burns up your body. Why anyone would eat pork cracklings if they want to lose weight is beyond me, but she must have thought the pills would counteract her craving. It's really very sad. Chloé said Wylène had been a perfectly healthy young woman, but she did like her *grattons*.

Apparently so much so that she couldn't live without them even in a wellness resort.'

Maman took another mouthful of creamy pasta, undeterred by her own off-putting story. 'Thing is, though,' she continued after she swallowed, 'Chloé is really quite upset. Can't you do something? You know... look into it?'

My mouth fell open. 'Mum! You of all people should know to let the police handle a case like this. Besides, I already promised I wasn't going to get involved. The last time someone asked me to investigate a murder, it didn't work out so well, remember? I just want to take my pictures and stay alive, really.' Had she forgotten about Franck's death threat? Though I knew I had to get on with my life if I didn't want to end up crying in the corner, scared of every shadow, it had taken quite a stern talking to myself after lunch to get me to leave the house. By myself. Exposed.

I was happy to have done it, since nothing had happened, and I now felt slightly more confident. But that didn't mean I was comfortable getting involved in more death, especially since I didn't see how I could be of any assistance without getting in the way of the official investigation.

'But there is no case! According to the police, the girl messed with the wrong chemicals. An accident, is what they say. But Chloé says Wylène wasn't into dieting at all. She was young, her metabolism able to work with anything she ate. And though she was pretty, she wasn't that vain. That's what Chloé says, anyway. She believes something is wrong.'

I looked my mother in the eye, choosing my words carefully. 'You don't think she could be influenced by the other murders happening on the same day? We don't always know everything about the people we care for. Or sometimes we choose not to know.'

I hoped she wouldn't take that as a critique of her behaviour after my father's death, when I got swept off my feet by Franck. I was actually talking about her 'appointments', though they, of course, weren't in any way dangerous.

Maman narrowed her eyes at me. Did she get it? 'Well... if you don't want to get involved, that's your right, of course. I'll have to talk to Thibault instead.'

'What? Why?' She'd done it again. Just when I thought I'd taken a stand, she bowled me over with an unexpected remark.

'Didn't you know? He was probably the last person to see Wylène alive. At least, he was seen at the Centre around the time we were on our hike. Is he upstairs?' She pointed over her shoulder in the direction of my studio.

'*Non.*' It was possibly the shortest sound I'd ever produced. Perhaps *Maman* was entitled to more of an explanation, but other than a raised eyebrow, she didn't ask, and I wasn't willing to expand. I really shouldn't be miffed about her wanting to talk to Beau, but she'd hit more than one sore spot with a single blow.

She thanked me for lunch but didn't repeat her appeal for help. I tried to infuse my goodbyes with a bit more affection, but when I trudged across the courtyard to my studio, I could almost see the dark cloud above my head. I could certainly feel its cold mist in my neck. Shivering, I entered my studio but then leant against the door and put my thumb and forefinger to my temple. Worry and jealousy and fear were not going to help me. I pulled them out of my head, opened the door, and flung the unwanted emotions out.

Now that my dark cloud had turned white (I mean, this thought-pulling can only do so much – sunshine would have been too much to ask), I could focus on editing the pictures I'd taken of Marie and her friends. Right after I'd done an internet search for the Centre de Prédiction.

Ignoring the sensible part of me that told me to work instead of being nosy, I typed in my search string, and up popped the website for the Centre, asking me if I wanted to go to the website for the physical centre or the virtual spa in the metaverse. Of course. A virtual spa was naturally part of this out-there wellness centre. Why hadn't I thought of that? Would anyone visit a virtual photographer? Do this to pose and then take a selfie. Hm, I'd stick to real-life photography. While I wanted to know about the real-life centre, I was intrigued enough to click the metaverse button. Soothing artists' impressions of what the perfect spa would be floated behind an explanation in an ethereal font of what I was visiting. For everyone unable to physically join 'us' in the Centre de Prédiction, here was a place to relax, listen to special music, and escape your daily sorrows. At check-in, you would be able to create an avatar to enjoy this perfect life in a perfect body. All this at a reduced fee. What a bargain.

I clicked through all the sessions that were included in the price, and some that could be added as extras. And then there was the merch, again both physical and metaphysical, which your digital self could show off. I wondered if anyone would be crazy enough to buy into this, but according to the sneak peek, there were plenty of people milling about in the virtual lounge, their imaginative name tags displayed above their heads.

SkyRider34, a black male avatar, was trying to scale one of the organic, white shapes that made up the walls to this space, while in the flowerbed next to him, Peru_Girl was making snow angels, the flowers disappearing and reappearing as she passed over them with her arms and legs. I12L0V3U was trying to talk to a blonde woman reading a book on an airbed floating in a tiny pond that seemed to travel with her. Quiet!AmReading was obviously not interested in his advances. He should have known.

As fascinating as this scene was, it wasn't what I'd come for, so I clicked out of the metaCentre to return to the part of the website dedicated to real life. 'Our Vision' drew my eye. I'd have been blind to miss it, really, as it was the biggest thing on the screen. A video of the man in the white durag-turban I'd seen yesterday appeared and started playing.

'Welcome. Peace.' The Zen music playing in the background was already starting to get on my nerves, or maybe it was the silky quality of the man's voice. 'Let go of your worries. Say goodbye to frustration. Let us help you become what you were always meant to be. Worthy. In control. The future is yours. Come to the Centre de Prédiction and let me show you.'

He pressed his hands together and bowed his namaste to the camera, while I suppressed a gag reflex. I could tell the future right now. He would be richer and whoever fell for this would be poorer. Nothing wrong with trying to find some peace and quiet in your soul, but these prices made my photographic experiences look cheap. And the customer didn't even come away with a conversation-piece memento. Unless they stole the robe.

I quickly flicked through the list of famous and wannabe-famous guests before I'd had enough. My cursor already hovered over the little cross in the corner, when I spotted something familiar in the background of one of the photos. Behind the smiling face of an up-and-coming actress in a white, fluffy robe was a pedestal on which sat one of Jessica's spiky statues. I clicked the cross, then stared unseeingly at my desktop screen.

It was a link. A far-fetched one, perhaps. Maybe just the local connection. Very likely coincidental. But it stuck in my mind even after I'd opened my files to select the pictures I would work on. Half an hour later, I realised I'd been staring at Moira's thigh for several minutes already, without doing anything with it. I was trying hard not to think about any of the recent deaths, but the trying kept my mind so occupied that I couldn't think of anything else either. Sighing, I gave up. I might as well have a good think about all this and put my thoughts in order so I could focus on more important matters.

Switching off the screen for a moment, I grabbed the pen and paper I kept on the desk for quick sketches. Now, a list. Every half-formed thought that had been trying to take shape should be on this list, so I could truly think them and then get rid of them.

Firstly, I still hadn't heard from Thibault. *That* was number one? Thanks, brain, you really know how to pick 'em. But now that I'd mentioned it, I was worried. Beau often went away without telling me where, which was no more than logical. It was none of my business where he was out of hours. But to go for more than a day without receiving some kind of message, even just a forwarded meme or clip of someone falling on their face, was unusual. And since he'd been angry when he left, and his leaving coincided with Franck's release, I was more than a little worried.

Number two, Franck's release. No surprise that he was high on the list. Where was he? Was he planning something? Something bad? To do with me? My pen hovered and I lifted my head. As I sat up straight, I placed my pen on the paper, and a big smile spread across my face. Franck came second! I was more worried about Beau than about Franck. In fact, I wasn't scared of Franck at all. I was worried about what his release might do to Beau, but to me? All right, maybe I was a little scared still. However, it was more the uncertainty of whether I should be scared or not that frightened me. I was fearing fear. How unexpectedly wise of me.

Feeling quite smug, I picked up my pen again, finally turning to what I'd meant to write. Three deaths in one day: a personal assistant, a painter, and an art dealer. The art dealer and the painter had both been murdered, and the art made an obvious second link between them. But what about the young assistant? The police treated her death as self-inflicted, but her boss denied that. If *Maman* asked me to investigate, Chloé must think there was another party involved. Another murder? On the same day?

My third point on the list was a question: are all three murders linked? Same killer?

If it was, they'd had a prolific day. Actually, that was probably a good note to take. Who came when? Of course, I'd heard about Wylène first, but in fact, it was probably Xavier who died first. Some time after ten, according to Jessica. And Wylène likely died somewhere between half past ten and half past eleven, during our walk. I'd have to ask Jacqueline to confirm that timeline, but she wasn't likely to tell me. Wasn't I meant to stay away from this?

Ignoring myself once more, I put the third victim on my list: the painter. He'd died some time after two, because nobody had noticed police cars when they came to my party. Actually, that only meant he hadn't been found until after two. But he probably died later than the others. Besides that, I didn't know anything about him.

That was the problem with all of it. I didn't know anything. How could my mother ask me to look into this if I didn't know anything? And did I even want to? In order not to have to answer that question, I switched on my monitor and was confronted with Moira's thigh. Moira had mentioned that she'd smuggled some crisps into the Centre. I wondered how hard that had been...

Switching windows from Moira's thigh to Moira's phone number in my business records, I tapped it into my phone but then hesitated. I could ask her directly, but she might also be my way into the Centre, if I could think of something I couldn't ask over the phone. Now that I knew there was at least one of Jessica's artworks there, I was dying to have a look inside, but they had a policy in place that forbade anyone but guests to enter the building. Something about disturbing the experience of peace and calm. With all the police milling about yesterday, they were bound to be extra strict about that rule now. Would I even be allowed in as a guest of a guest?

Since Chloé had asked *Maman* to ask me to investigate, she would be the natural person to visit, but I also didn't feel like being stuck comforting someone I hardly knew, like *Maman* had been. Before I could second-guess myself, I called Moira.

'Hi, it's Julie Belmain.'

'I know! I'm so glad you called. Marie told me about you and the murders, and we have had such an interesting shake-up here. So yesterday—'

'Before you tell me all about it, do you think there's any way I could come visit you at the Centre?'

She was quiet for half a second, then her voice sounded amused. 'Ohhh, I seee! Absolutely. They don't normally allow visitors, but I'll just tell them you're my emotional support person, or something. After the commotion yesterday, they can hardly deny me someone to restore my inner peace, right? Leave it to me. I'll see you soon.'

Wow. That was easy. Of course, I wasn't in yet, but for some reason, I had no doubt Moira would manage that. And I didn't even need her thigh. Shutting down my computer, I shushed the voice telling me this was not what I should be doing. Had Moira not just given me permission to not work on her thigh? Perhaps not directly, but I could certainly take it that way. And I wasn't getting in the way of the police, because they said it was an accident and weren't investigating.

There – I'd cleared my conscience.

11

There, there

The moss green, undulating glass walls of the Centre de Prédiction glimmered in the sunlight. It wasn't the only big building in the area, far from it. The Château de Montmales was at least as big, especially if you counted its grounds. But the Château, like all the other big *domaines*, was built from the local yellow stone, melding into the landscape despite having a different shape. The clinical cleanness of the glass and gold Centre stuck out like a sore thumb. They'd probably have a remedy for that inside, though.

When I tried to enter, I was immediately stopped by an efficient-looking lady in a lab coat, her hair twisted into a tight topknot. 'Excuse me, this building is for guests only.'

'How do you know I'm not a guest?'

She looked down her nose at my petticoat-supported poodle skirt. 'You're not wearing a robe.'

Quite the giveaway, I had to admit. 'I'm here for Moira MacAdams.'

Another suspicious glance at the poodle. Maybe I should have worn something slightly more professional, but why couldn't I be a psychologist with style?

'I see. Wait here, I shall inform her.'

'Please do.' I tried to mimic her haughty look, knowing full well I could never find that much disdain inside of me. She was already negating the calming effect the building was supposed to have. But then, the calming effect was for paying guests, of course, which I was clearly not. Still, by the time Moira came hurrying around the corner, I'd almost dozed off. The egg-white, organic shapes that were everywhere from chairs to lampshades to the reception desk, paired with the faint sound of waves caressing a beach, must have got to me. I hadn't thought the strange colour on the walls would have been that effective in relaxing me. The pale aubergine-y mauve-taupe mix they'd used might have looked good on the sample, but being surrounded by it made me feel like I was swimming in a wilted lavender soup.

Moira's black hair stood out from her head, as if she'd been pulling it in all directions. Tears streaming down her cheeks, she fell into my arms. 'Julieheeheeheee, I'm so glad you're here! I can't deal… I can't. I'm supposed to…'

'There, there.' I patted her awkwardly on her head. Does anyone ever say 'there, there'? I was the world's worst actress. 'Let's go to your room, so you can tell me all about it.' Yep, the worst. If lab coat lady wasn't going to throw me right back out, that showed her lack of judgement better than my talents. Before she could do just that, I led Moira past her, trying not to feel her squinty gaze on the back of my head.

As soon as we'd rounded the corner, Moira straightened and combed a hand through her hair. 'There, there?' She laughed softly, so as not to raise suspicion. 'Wow.'

I gave her an embarrassed smile and a shrug. 'You took me by surprise. I didn't know if I was supposed to be a friend or some kind of professional.'

'Doesn't matter. Neither would have said "there, there".' She shook her head with a grin. 'But you're in, so what do you want to know?'

I grinned back. Moira was quite an attack on the senses, but I could see why Marie liked her so much. 'You'll be happy to hear this is none of my business, but I'm sticking my nose in anyway.' Why kid myself? I'd already solved three murders. Maybe this is what I should be doing. Ordinarily, I had to stop Beau from barging in, but since he wasn't involved this time...

Moira made an appreciative noise and nodded as she opened one of the many white doors tinged green from the glass wall opposite.

'You already know about the death here,' I told her, 'but there were two more yesterday. Both murders. Now the companion of the girl who died here thinks her death is suspicious too.'

Waving me into a white leather chair, Moira sat on the bed, one leg tucked underneath. 'Well, I can tell you, this place has been buzzing with theories. We all know the official version with the pork cracklings and the diet pills, because we had to submit to room searches. "Unprecedented circumstances", is what they gave as a justification. Got a stink eye from the orderly for my crisps, but as it turns out, I was far from the only one who'd brought in "sinful" food from the outside. If that's sin, I'd rather not be a saint. But this place is much less fun without crisps, I can tell you. I was actually thinking of leaving to stay with Marie instead when you called.'

Pouting like a toddler who'd been told off for smashing a toy, she glared at the built-in cupboard that I surmised had once contained the coveted crisps.

'So... what theories?'

'Oh! Ha! I've heard everything from suicide to cowboys.'

'Cowboys?' Now that theory I had to hear.

Moira rolled her eyes. 'Never mind that one. There's a woman here, Kiki Sandhomme, who always says the most outrageous things. First she thought it was lye, then she'd somehow worked out there were cowboys involved. I don't believe a word she says, but I stay with her like a shadow, just to be entertained by the next thing she'll come up with.'

'Sandhomme...' I pursed my lips. 'That's not a name you hear every day.'

'But you know it?'

I chuckled. Not much escaped this one. 'I met another Sandhomme this afternoon. An artist.' Thought that was worth mentioning with all the other art connections. But Moira shrugged.

'I don't know anything about art. They have stuff lying around here, but to me, that's just clutter. Kiki did mention going to visit her daughter, though, so maybe that's her?' She shrugged again. 'Lots of artists around here. That's actually the one thing I talked to that dead girl about.'

I looked up. Moira had met Wylène? 'Oh?'

'Yes, she was nice. Sweet face. She saw me come in with that painting when I'd just bought it.' She inclined her head towards a board leaning against the wall in a corner. It was back-to-front, so I couldn't see the picture. 'My dad likes that kind of stuff, especially if it's local to somewhere I've travelled. He never likes to leave home, so... Anyway, I came in and she asked if I'd got it in Villefranche, but I'd picked it up at a ceramics market in Jarnioux.'

I knew that place. A ceramics market is what the artists from the nearby commune called it, but since that's where they all sold their wares, there were always some people selling paintings or textile art. On a sunny day, it was a lovely spot to have a nose around before spreading a picnic on the field behind it, near the playground. With the sounds of kids playing and the colourful stalls of the artists in the background, you could have a two-hour holiday there.

'She said she'd bought her painting in Villefranche,' Moira continued, 'but that the artist was long dead, so it couldn't be the same one. I really didn't have anything to say to that, so we said goodbye. I'm sorry she's gone, though.'

We sat in silence for a while. Her words reminded me that maybe I shouldn't be so curious about this whole affair after all. I wasn't a curious person, normally. What on Earth had made me want to get involved this time? It must be because Thibault had left. Or my mother had asked me. Either of them was to blame, not me. I'd better leave before I got in too deep and Jacqueline had to kick me out.

'Do you have a spare robe? I'd like to have a look at the artworks.' Well, I was here, wasn't I? Might as well have a look around. That didn't mean I was looking for murderers.

Moira provided me with a robe, but since she wasn't interested in the art, I ventured out into the hallway by myself. After several minutes of wandering, I'd still only seen the same nondescript, white swirls that could have come from the local bargain store. The art here was apparently not meant to intrude upon the calm of the surroundings. That made sense around here, but I knew I'd seen Jessica's art in that online photo.

'Julie?'

I hastily tuned from the door marked 'Private' that I'd been about to open. 'Chloé! How are you?' Sliding on my most sympathetic mask, I stretched my hands out to her, but when I saw her lip wobble, my fake concern turned genuine. She had lost a good friend, after all. I might not look forward to being stuck with her, but who else did she have?

'I keep going back and forth between disbelief and desperation,' she said, wringing her hands. Over her robe, she'd slung the same shoulder bag she'd worn when we went on our hike. 'Monsieur Othman here has been extremely forthcoming, for which I am intensely grateful.' She indicated the man in white I hadn't even noticed, but who now took a step forward with a slight bow.

'Anything to guide you through this most difficult time, so you can find your inner strength again.' His face turned a shade less compassionate when he turned to me. 'I don't believe I've had the pleasure of making your acquaintance yet, though I make it a point to welcome all my guests personally.'

Whoops! Time to channel my inner Thibault. This was usually when he found the perfect answer while I turned into a beetroot. I'd have to be more convincing now, so I hoped my blood would stay put and not rise to my cheeks. 'I came here yesterday, just after the tragedy. You did see me, but I think you had more pressing matters to attend to.' That wasn't even a lie! Beau could be proud. If he ever came back…

Monsieur Othman narrowed his eyes slightly but then cast down his gaze. 'My apologies for not giving you my full attention. I shall make sure to rectify the oversight.'

Was it me, or was that a veiled threat? I was still in front of the door accusingly marked 'Private'. Attack seemed the best defence here, so I asked, 'I seem to remember seeing a photo on your website that showed some interesting art?'

His eyebrows shot up. 'Ah, you are interested in the healing power of beauty and expression.' Did he ever stop? 'Chloé? Will you be all right while I show Julie our collection?'

Pushing her hair behind her ear, Chloé straightened. 'I'd like to come, too, if you don't mind. I need all the healing power I can get.'

'Of course.' He surprised me by seeming genuine in his softness towards her as he guided us through the mauve-taupe corridors to a larger space, where not only the walls, but also the ceiling were curved. This must be the room inside the golden ball, as there were no windows and the entire space was artificially lit. The walls here were black, but white pedestals holding sculptures and white screens supporting paintings seemed haphazardly placed around the floor. The effect was visually pleasing nonetheless, as if all the art was doing a kind of dance together.

Chloé entered first but then hesitated, as if she wasn't sure which piece to approach first. She opened her purse and took out a pair of brown gloves, probably to avoid any kind of damage to the artworks. I sidestepped her and made a beeline for the spiky work at the centre. 'This is interesting.'

A small smile played on Monsieur Othman's lips. 'You have a good eye. This particular artist is very sought after. I was lucky to be able to get one of her works before they became unaffordable.'

'It does seem somewhat out of place, though,' I remarked. 'It isn't very soothing.'

His smile grew but he kept it within bounds. 'An astute observation. That is precisely its purpose here – to draw out whatever emotions lie beneath the surface. Our guests come here to subconsciously choose what emotions they need to address. You went straight for a piece that represents anger and frustration, which suggests you should book a session with Talía.'

I pressed my lips together, and he gave a soft chuckle. Against my better judgement, the sound drew me in, and I smiled.

He took me gently by the elbow and showed me a sweet painting of children playing on the shore. 'If you're attracted to darker pieces, how do you feel about this one?'

I peered at it. 'Why, is there a shark in the water?'

He laughed out loud at that, and more of my hostility melted away. Perhaps I had been too quick to judge.

'No, nothing horrific like that. I merely meant to contrast this classically painted scene with the sculpture that drew you to it. Would you say this was to your liking?'

I studied the painting and decided it was. I liked how the artist had skilfully capped the waves with white froth, and how the beach looked sandy even though the paint wasn't applied in dots, which is what I would have done. Even the serene tranquillity of the scene appealed to me. But since Monsieur Othman now thought I was a secret barbarian, I wasn't sure how to react.

'Oh, I have one of his.' Chloé saved me from having to answer by pointing her leather-clad finger rather too close to the signature on the painting in front of me. 'Bought it only two days ago, from that nice man in Villefranche.'

Her declaration had me inspect the signature, and my eyes widened. Régis Piguemal, the same name as on the painting Gilles had given me. So there had also been happy paintings like this one, but I had an aggressive one. 'This painting annoys me,' I could honestly say to the man in white beside me.

His smile had disappeared, but he nodded slowly. 'We all have our own versions of reality, because we see it through the lenses of our experiences and character traits. If we let it, art can bring out both our pleasure and our pain. I believe it's essential to understand our pain before we can open ourselves up to any of the healing therapies on offer. Once you identify your pain, I predict you will have less of it in the future. Less pain means more energy to put towards your pleasure.'

Though he'd probably repeated this spiel time and time again, it didn't sound so outrageous any more. Perhaps he actually had a point. Taking me by the shoulders, he turned me towards another painting, this one depicting a forest, or rather, a collection of brown tree trunks. I'd seen something similar in the home of Apolline Bailly, one of the village's notables and no particular friend of mine. 'Now, this artist is quite polarising. Some love his work, some hate it. But what emotion does it call up for you?'

Loneliness. But since I wasn't sure if it was the painting that made me uncomfortable or the association with Apolline, I searched for something else in the image, preferably something positive this time.

'Power in numbers,' Chloé answered for me. She pushed around me to get closer to the art.

Maybe I should introduce her to Apolline, I thought as I stepped out of her way. In doing so, I half-turned and caught a wince on Monsieur Othman's face. He schooled his expression when he saw me notice, but then took a deep breath.

'Forgive me. As much as I love my collection, today, it also brings me great sorrow. My dearest friend, my soulmate when it came to art, passed only yesterday, quite unexpectedly. Beholding these works, and contemplating the memories attached, brings me more pain than pleasure at the moment.'

'Oh.' Fingers on her lips, Chloé turned from the painting and placed her other hand on his arm. The gesture was so intimate that I thought it best to silently back away and let them share their grief in private.

Closing the door behind me, I hurried back to Moira's room.

'Are you all right?' she asked as I entered. 'You look a little pale.'

'To be honest, I'm not sure. I ran into Monsieur Othman and—'

Moira burst out laughing. 'You're certainly not the only one he's managed to bowl over. You should see the little faces of people after they've been welcomed by his charming pitch. It's a form of entertainment all on its own. You'd have to be as cynical as me not to fall for it, which you are obviously not. Trust me, it'll pass. Or not, since you're not paying.' She sent me a wink, and I quickly changed back into my normal clothes.

Had I really been so gullible? That would be the second time today, after Maile's story. But Othman had seemed authentic. Especially when he'd mentioned Xavier. Or, his friend. I assumed he meant Xavier because of the art, but he never actually named him. Hm. Had I actually found out anything by coming here, or had it been a mistake to try and find out anything to begin with?

My confusion had only partly cleared up by the time I reached my house. I was once again certain that Monsieur Othman's grief had been genuine, but my emotions were still on an arty rollercoaster. In an attempt to set my feelings right, I picked up my new painting and put it flat on my kitchen table. Well, my first thought was still 'yuck', so I must not be that shook up after all. But did that mean Othman's vision had got to me?

My stomach rumbled, giving me the perfect scapegoat. Once I'd eaten, all would be well. I would see the world clearly once more with my belly full. What to eat, though? I had enough ingredients lying around to make a variety of things, but I was hungry *now*. I'd become used to cooking for Beau too, but since it was just me once more... Clearly, the solution was to visit Theo, the chef at Jeanette Ta's café. He made a *salade Lyonnaise* that was just the thing.

Switching to kitten heels for the walk into the village, I also grabbed a cardigan. April days in the Beaujolais had the best temperatures in my opinion, but the nights could still be chilly as the sun set early. And though I was convinced nothing would happen to me after I'd realised Franck came second to Beau in my catalogue of worries, I still shivered and rubbed my arms as I hurried along the road. All was dark in Anne-Bonny's house, as well as in Tiana's when I glanced up the hill. David's Grande Maison did have a light on downstairs, but since I could only see the ceiling from the street below, that didn't make me feel much less alone.

Should I send Thibault a message? Maybe I should apologise, but for what? Ask if there was something I could do? What I actually wanted to know was what was wrong, but what if that should have been obvious from his point of view? It would only make him more angry with me. If he was angry with me. True, his words had felt like a rejection, like Jessica's art was somehow better than mine, so maybe I'd been a bit sharp towards him after that, but that couldn't be his reason for staying away. Could it?

In fact, I had more reason to be angry with him than the other way round. He had not been there yesterday, at three, when I'd needed him as a friend. To show me that Franck was the only rotten apple in his family, not one of a bunch. My stomach squeezed together with a familiar flicker of doubt. Had I been taken by this family yet again? Now that Franck was free, would Thibault show his true colours?

I thought of Beau's mother, whom I'd met on a few occasions. She was a lovely woman. But she was married to a man who'd stayed loyal to his brother Franck to this day. I'd always thought Beau and his mother were on my side, but how could I be sure of that?

I breathed a sigh of relief when Jeanette's café came into view. The customers who'd chosen a table outside so they could smoke were a welcome sight as they chatted and laughed over their glasses of wine. Me, I preferred to be inside today. Looking around to see if any of my friends were in, I saw a red-headed woman wave at me. The one with the better art. Did I want to sit there?

Oh, now I was just being childish. It wasn't Jessica's fault that Beau had left. Nor that he apparently thought her art was preferable to mine. I smiled and joined her at the table she shared with Alain.

'I'm not intruding, am I?'

'Would I have waved you over if you were? Sit, sit. I wanted to apologise for this afternoon. I was a little... frustrated.'

Jeanette served me a glass of local red in passing, winking to let me know she'd be back for my order. She knew I didn't need a menu. She kept a few for tourists, but all the locals knew the specials by heart.

'You're under investigation for murder. I think I can forgive you for not being all too charming right now.'

'I think she's perfectly charming already,' our handsome companion declared, laying it on a little too thickly for my liking, but Jessica giggled.

'Alain has been a life saver. I mean, we only met yesterday, but he's been so patient with me. And I've had a few rants, believe me.'

Sipping my wine, I glanced between the two of them. That same feeling of suspicion that had crept up on me this afternoon surfaced once more. 'Yes, you mentioned your rather short acquaintance. But why are you here?' I addressed Alain bluntly to gauge his reaction, but nothing in his demeanour changed from the relaxed man enjoying a dinner with friends. 'I mean, Jessica's studio is not exactly a logical place to end up.'

'You're right, it's not,' he said with an engaging smile. 'I got lucky. I finished one project and didn't have another lined up, so I got on the first bus I found, rode it to its terminal, and started walking. I figured that was as good a method of finding a new challenge as any.'

Except maybe searching on the internet or asking around? 'What kind of project are you looking for?'

Jeanette chose that moment to take my order, which gave him time to think of an answer. Then again, he must have already thought of one when Jessica asked him. Although she gave him her full attention as well. But was that because she found him fascinating and hoped for more information, or because in all the commotion she hadn't even asked him herself yet?

'I'm a kind of entrepreneur.' *Kind of?* As attractive as he was, his vagueness wasn't making him very popular in my eyes. Which is probably why he focussed on the adoring eyes of my neighbour. 'I find a struggling business, make it work, and then I move on.'

'Jessica is not a struggling business.'

He turned back to me, but where I expected him to sneer or deflect, his gaze was open and perhaps even amused, when he answered, 'No, but a large part of the building she's in isn't used right now. It may be isolated, but its layout has potential.'

'Potential for what?'

At that point, Jessica groaned. 'Julie, come on! What's with the third degree? He wanted to stay in a hotel and come back the next day, I said that made no sense and he was welcome to stay the night, and that was all. I already asked him if he was an axe murderer and he said no. In fact, he's been brilliant since I met him. He talked to the police to make them go away, and he's found me a new dealer. Even though Anaëlle said she could probably have found me some buyers.'

Ah, yes, the grumpy friend who didn't believe Jessica was innocent. 'And how long have you known her?'

'Julie!' Jessica rolled her eyes. 'You're not the police. Actually, they came by again this afternoon, after you left. Apparently, Xavier's secretary called them like one minute after ten, so now they really don't believe I saw him drive off at ten. He didn't say it, but you could just see that guy think, "If that's not true, then none of it is true." They think I did it, but I saw him drive off! I know he did. That secretary must be the one lying. Maybe she did it.'

She threw her hands in the air and shook her copper curls. As much as I felt for her, though, my attention was drawn to Alain, whose carefree veneer finally showed some cracks. An echo of his earlier smile still hung around his lips, but his eyes were on Jessica. The wheels were clearly turning, but I couldn't make out in which direction.

As if he felt my stare on him, his eyes glazed over before he turned to me with that same carefree attitude he'd been displaying all along. 'I'm sure it'll all work out. Some crazy artist is going to claim this was his masterpiece or something, and by next week, you'll be back to modelling clay.' Realising he'd laid back too far when Jessica frowned, he quickly added, 'I'm just saying, worrying about it isn't going to help. We have to trust that the police will do their job well. Like Julie said this afternoon.'

Forcing my eyes not to narrow at him, I nodded. As Jeanette came to the table with our orders, I had a few moments to come up with an answer. Something that wasn't 'Who are you, anyway? You're fake and I don't trust you.' Though those were the words I really wanted to say. The fact that he'd shown up moments after Xavier had died was too convenient. It had to be more than a coincidence. Maybe he hadn't planned it all out the way it happened, but why was he interested in exactly the building Jessica was in? The building that happened to be owned by the murdered man?

'I don't know what to think any more,' Jessica said after swallowing some of her *gougères*, cheese puffs that Théo managed to make both crispy and light while full of flavour. 'I know pretty much all the artists Xavier dealt with and I don't see them killing anyone. But he was one of those guys that gets a deal out of everything – construction, art, energy... Whatever he thought could make him money usually did in the end. But, you know, he cheated me, so he probably did that to others as well. I can't believe the police suspect me when there are so many other candidates out there.'

Her words faded in my ears, as though she were talking to me in a snowy landscape. Something was wrong, and I'd sensed it before I could consciously name it. The back of my neck started to tingle and everything around me slowed down. Somehow, I registered that Alain was the first to notice the change in me and that he immediately lost every bit of his nonchalance in favour of a primed alertness, but I knew – just *knew* – he was not my concern. This heart rate raising, blood curdling anxiety could only ever be linked to one man. Franck was here.

12

I have to talk to the capitaine

Outside, a gunshot sounded. While everyone around me stopped talking, my vision blurred. No! I had to stay with it. If Franck was here for me, I would fight!

The door slammed open, and in stumbled Thibault, clawing at his motorcycle helmet. He fell to one knee, fumbling with the strap. I was halfway out of my seat when a strong hand around my arm held me back. Pushing me back in my seat, Alain rushed forward. With his arm around Beau, he led him away from the glass door towards our table, before taking off the helmet.

Seeing Beau's face, pale and wide-eyed but unharmed, almost had me lose consciousness again. But then he spotted me. There was a moment's hesitation where he tensed and I thought he was going to walk away, but then his shoulders lowered and he looked me in the eye.

'I'm sorry.'

It took me a few seconds to remember what he was apologising for, and after what just happened, it seemed ridiculous for *that* to be the first thing on his mind.

'Who cares! Are you all right?'

He opened his mouth, but Jeanette Ta pushed Alain aside to shove a glass of water in Beau's hand. 'Police are on their way. Here, sit.' She waved me out of my chair and rammed it in the back of Beau's knees. Water sloshed over the edge of the glass as he landed on the chair, but he spoke calmly, 'I'm okay. Don't worry, they didn't get me.'

'Killed your helmet, though.' Alain showed us all the double hole in the shiny, black surface, one side dappled with bits of polystyrene.

Thibault snatched the helmet from his hand. 'Aw, man! This was my favourite.' But his frown deepened in the silence that followed as we all blinked at his priorities and he seemed to realise the triviality of what he'd just said.

Both hands clasped over her heart, Jessica finally found her voice. 'But why are people shooting at you?'

I took a deep breath before I softly said, 'Perhaps you were right to leave.' I didn't want him to. He'd been gone for two days, and I'd missed him more than I wanted to admit, but there was only one reason why anyone would shoot at him. Me.

But Beau put his water on the table, stood up, and slowly turned to me, dripping disdain on my ignorance. 'Obviously not.'

He looked like he was about to make me the target of some pent-up frustration, when the door slammed open a second time. The first thing I saw was Jacqueline's astonished face, because Céline had moved so fast that I hadn't even registered that she'd pushed past the scary policewoman to get to Beau, whom she was now frantically patting down.

'Thibault, I heard you were shot! Are you okay?'

Thrown by her sudden appearance, Beau stared at the baker's daughter still searching for holes. 'Shot *at*.' He took her hands in his and held them on his chest until she looked him in the eyes. 'I'm fine.'

'Really?' She clutched his shirt and didn't let go when he repeated the words.

Slowly, some colour returned to Beau's cheeks, and he produced a wavery version of his signature smile. Céline only frowned at it, and he sighed. 'I'll be all right. I have to talk to the *capitaine*.'

'Yes, you do,' Jacqueline confirmed.

Céline reluctantly let go of Beau's shirt, but directed her frown at Jacqueline. 'I thought you're a homicide detective. Has someone else been killed?'

'Not today.' Jacqueline gave her head a short shake. 'But this café is right next to the church, which is the scene of an ongoing murder investigation, so when there's gunfire in an otherwise peaceful village and I happen to be in the neighbourhood... Though I'm starting to doubt that's a true description of Saint-Maurice in the first place. Thibault, it would be very useful if you could tell us who shot at you. I don't suppose you saw...?'

Beau cast down his gaze by way of answer, and Jacqueline sighed. 'Looks like they got away unseen. I have a few people out there questioning everyone who was outside at the time, so maybe we'll get more than "someone on a motorcycle, possibly female", but it's not looking too hopeful.'

She paused, giving Beau time to volunteer any information he had, but when nothing came, she continued, 'All right, let's move to somewhere more private. Is there a back room in this establishment?'

I shook my head. 'Maybe we can go to mine?'

'Yes,' Beau agreed. 'Let's go home.'

I did my best not to show it, but his words warmed my heart. We'd have plenty to talk about, but at least he still considered my house his home.

Jacqueline nodded. 'We might as well. And you are...?' She turned to my companions at the table.

'Alain Coquard. We just happened to be dining together.'

'Jessica Rose. I'm afraid we didn't see anything until Thibault came in.'

Herding Beau and me towards the door, Jacqueline nodded again. 'Please speak to one of my officers. I'm afraid I'll have to break up your dinner.'

I managed a little wave before we were womanhandled out the door and into Jacqueline's car. Since she was quiet on the short drive over, neither Beau nor I spoke. He probably needed some time to get over being a target, and I simply didn't know where to start. Did I welcome him back? Express concern over what just happened? Or what had happened before?

Jacqueline parked in my driveway, and I let us all into my kitchen, making coffee for what I presumed would be quite the conversation.

'Look, I hate to bring your family and your past into this, but unless I'm very much mistaken, this has absolutely nothing to do with the murder in the church. Now you tell me what it *is* about.'

Apparently, Jacqueline didn't think being shot at warranted a soft approach. At least not with Beau. He didn't seem to mind too much, but with the way he sat slouched on the kitchen chair, staring at his hands, he reminded me of a sulking teenager. I put a mug in front of him and squeezed his shoulder, not sure what else I could do to show my support.

'I... don't know.'

'That's helpful.'

'What? I don't know!' At least he was looking at her now.

'You know *something*. People don't just get shot at around here. Especially you.'

'Have you considered that my uncle is out of jail and he may not like it very much that I'm living with his ex-wife who put him in jail in the first place?'

'So he's going to shoot you and not her?'

Both their voices had gone up in volume during their exchange, but having them talk about me as if I wasn't there annoyed me. 'He was there.'

They both stared at me, slightly confused. Yes, I was indeed still here.

'Who?' Jacqueline asked.

'Franck. I didn't see him – not consciously, anyway – but he was there. I got cold all over, right before I heard the shot. I had my back to the door and only turned round when Beau came in, which means Franck was inside the café when Beau was shot outside, but his presence must be related.'

Jacqueline pursed her lips but didn't agree. 'Did you see him?' she asked Beau.

'I was a bit preoccupied.' He was now staring at the coffee in his hands.

Stirring and sipping our coffee, we sat in silence around the kitchen table for a while.

'So that's your story,' Jacqueline said at last.

Beau let out a frustrated sigh. 'First the girl I'm with dies. Then I get shot. Who am I, James Bond?'

Despite the situation, I snorted. 'At least the bad guys have the same terrible aim.'

His eyebrows shot up, but then, for the first time that evening, he showed a genuine grin. 'Watch out, MI6. There's a new spy in town.' He folded his hands into a gun and pointed at me. 'Fouquet, Thibault Fouquet.'

'Shaken and disturbed.' My laugh died when I saw Jacqueline's face.

'Excuse me while I try to do my job here.' She turned to Beau. 'Why did you bring up Wylène Chiche? You said she hadn't told you anything.'

'Wait.' I straightened. 'You talked to him?'

'Of course. He was one of the last people to see Madame Chiche alive.'

I knew it was ridiculous, but I had to keep my lip from jutting into a pout. If Jacqueline had found it strange that she'd had to talk to him anywhere else but here, she kept that to herself.

'So?' she prompted Beau.

'I didn't do much…' he started, but after an audible intake of breath from Jacqueline, he hastily expanded. 'You said it was an accident, that she'd taken diet pills, but we talked all night and not once did she mention anything about her weight, or the way she looked, or whatever. It just didn't seem to fit, so I asked around a bit. Like we did before, *tu sais*?' He waved his hand between me and him.

'In other words, you snooped.'

He shrugged. 'What? You said it was an accident, so I assumed you were done investigating.'

Again, my lip was in danger of jutting. He'd gone sleuthing without me. 'So who did you talk to?'

'That's what I'd like to know,' Jacqueline added with a silencing glare at me.

Beau rubbed his forehead. 'Well, we mainly talked about art that night. She'd told me she bought a painting at Galerie Grosse, so that's where I went first, but it was closed.'

'She went to Xavier's place?' I blurted.

'We knew that,' Jacqueline said calmly – dare I say icily? – 'but it didn't seem related to her death.'

'You don't think that it's just a little bit of a coincidence that Wylène went to a guy who gets murdered and then she dies too?' But what seemed obvious to me didn't to Jacqueline. She was trying hard to stay professional and not shout at me to be quiet.

She took a deep breath. 'That's exactly what I think it is. Julie, we're trying to find out who shot your friend. Can we focus, please?'

Not wanting to seem insensitive, I let her do the asking and Beau the talking, but honestly, how could she not see the neon sign connecting all these deaths? Whoever was on this killing spree must also have it in for Beau, for some reason. If we could work out why the first three were killed, we'd have Beau's attacker too. If Jacqueline wasn't willing to listen, I'd have to talk to Beau about it myself, so I waited patiently for the interrogation to come to an unsatisfying close.

'None of those people sound like they'd want to shoot at you. But we will follow up, of course.'

'I told you already, I don't know. That's why.'

'Hm.' She finished her coffee and stood. Grabbing the phone she'd been making notes on, she made her way to the door, but turned when she reached it, looking at both of us in turn. 'If Franck was at the café, he can't have been the one to shoot. *Please*. Be careful.'

That hadn't occurred to me yet. But I'd have to worry about it in a minute. I had one more thing I wanted to ask.

'We will be. But can you tell me one unrelated thing?'

She narrowed her eyes.

'Xavier Grosse. Was he wearing his rings, and did he have his car keys?'

'Not my case. And not yours either, Julie. Stay out of trouble.'

13

I promised not to get involved

'Art has to be the connection somehow,' I told Beau as soon as Jacqueline had left.

He didn't answer.

Biting my lip for letting my brain get ahead of my compassion, I got up, rounded the table and hugged him from behind. He tensed at first but then relaxed and lifted one hand to stroke my arms resting on his chest.

'I'm so glad you're back.' I gave him one last squeeze, then released him and held up the coffee pot, which he shook his head at.

'I'm really sorry, Julie. I should have been at your party. But I... couldn't.'

'Wanna talk about it?'

'Would you let me get away with saying no?'

I filled my own cup and grinned. Even though I wasn't the curious kind, it was better for him to get it off his chest.

'I thought as much.' He drew a pattern on the table with his finger, staring at it when he said, 'I'd met Wylène in a bar in

Villefranche. She was with this older woman she introduced as her boss, but they acted more like friends. Bit strange.'

I pursed my lips but held my tongue. Who was he to judge an older woman boss who was also a friend? Perhaps there was another strange thing he was referring to.

'She was so smart. I mean, we talked about random things, but with each topic, she had one little thing to say that I didn't know, *tu sais*? Just that little bit more, that little bit deeper. I really liked her. The other woman left at some point. I kind of expected her to say something about working nights or something, but none of that. When I asked Wylène what she did, she said "business", and that was that. She didn't want to talk about work, so we talked about everything else. Bar closed, we kept talking. I took her to the lake because she didn't want to get back to the Centre de Prédiction just yet. I thought we could sit there for a while and I'd take her back at some point, but we kept finding more things to talk about. Mostly art. She was pretty passionate about that.'

He paused, and I took another sip of my drink, not wanting to disturb his memories.

'So at some point, I had to get back here. It was already late and I was dead tired by then. I offered to take her to the Centre, but she said she'd stay there and do some forest bathing, which I guess meant taking a nap, because when I got back there when you were on your walk, she was still asleep under the tree. She barely woke up enough for me to take her back to the Centre. The only thing she said after that was that she was hungry and she'd call me when she woke up. Next thing I know...'

He stopped, twisting the mug between his hands. I searched for words of comfort, but found none. He might have only known her for a short time, but the connection between them was obvious. To lose that connection before being able to explore it must leave more than a void. He was missing something without knowing what had been there. Loss and confusion made for a powerfully negative combination.

I reached over the table, and he took my hand without looking at it. 'Jacqueline came to me because someone had seen me take her to the Centre. They mentioned that she looked dazed, which made sense, since she'd hardly slept. Later, when they'd found the cause of death, Jacqueline called me again, to ask if Wylène had shown any signs of taking those pills earlier, as they couldn't find any trace of them in her room. Nor of the *grattons*. So I said we didn't have anything to eat but had shared a bottle of water. I also told her the pills didn't make sense, but she said she couldn't discuss that with me.'

'So you thought what I thought. There has to be a connection between these deaths.' He nodded, and I continued, 'So did you find out anything else?'

He shook his head. 'Did you?'

'I, err…' I studied my nails. 'I promised not to get involved.'

'You what?' He burst out laughing, which I took as my cue to get back to normal. We'd come back to his experience and his feelings about it later, but for now, he could do with some distraction.

'I'm not as nosy as you are, you know. I don't have this need to get involved. Of course, that was before I found all these things that don't add up.'

'Well, it's a good thing *I* didn't promise anything, *quoi*? What have you got?'

I beamed as I started summing up on my fingers. At some point, Beau would grow tired of being my assistant and leave for more exciting prospects, but that moment was not now.

'Murder one, Xavier Grosse, the art dealer in Villefranche. Murder two, which neither of us believe was an accident, in the Centre de Prédiction. Murder three—'

'There was a third?'

I stared at him and was about to ask, 'Where have you been?', but of course, he hadn't been. Here, anyway. 'Yes, a painter from the commune, murdered in our church.'

'Your church, you mean.'

'I just meant the church in our village.' Though technically, the funds to build it had been donated by my family a long time ago, or so I'd been told. There were a lot of stories surrounding my ancestors, and I did not believe all of them.

Or maybe I didn't care to, which might make me an ostrich putting my head in the sand, but it had all happened so long ago that I couldn't feel particularly guilty about any of those stories any more.

'So an art dealer, a personal assistant, and a painter,' Beau mused.

'All on the same day,' I added.

'The connection between the art dealer and the painter I get. Do you know if Xavier represented him?'

I wrinkled my nose. 'I wasn't supposed to investigate, remember? Also, this is the only one of the three cases that Jacqueline is on. She says Wylène was an accident, and her colleague is after Xavier's killer.'

'Ah yes, the guy who thinks Jessica did it. Idiot.'

'According to Jacqueline, he is perfectly capable and will come to the right conclusion.' Sort of. 'But I wonder if he found those rings...'

'Yeah, what was that all about? You asked Jacqueline about the car keys as well?'

Pushing my cold coffee to the side, I leaned over the table towards my co-conspirator. 'Jessica says she saw Xavier drive off, but she only recognised him by the big silver rings he always wore. This was at ten o'clock. Around the same time, his secretary found Xavier's body inside, so it couldn't have been him driving off, unless the secretary is lying. I think the killer took his rings and his car keys, and he meant for Jessica, or anyone else, to see him drive off.'

'So that everyone would think the murder happened later? But why?'

'The killer probably has an alibi for later. That's what it usually means.'

'*Oui*, in detective stories. It's a little far-fetched in real life.' Thibault got up to pour his cold coffee down the sink.

'It's what makes the most sense to me, but if you have a better explanation?' I folded my arms in front of me, waiting for his genius contribution though not expecting any.

'Do you even know if the rings and the keys are missing? No, or you wouldn't have asked Jacqueline about it. It's an interesting idea, nothing more. So, like I said, I see the connection between the painter and the art dealer, but why do you think Wylène's death is related as well?'

Interesting idea, *hein*? Maybe I shouldn't tell him my ideas about Wylène's death if all they were going to be were interesting ideas. But since he would have to do my investigating for me in this case, I'd have to share my thoughts. 'She and Chloé, her boss, had bought a painting from Xavier the day before. Now, I don't think that was one of the dead painter's works since she told Moira her painting was done by someone long dead, but there is definitely a connection there. Also, the

Centre's owner was a good friend of Xavier's. He told me so when he showed me the art.'

'You went to the Centre.' Beau was doing a terrible job of keeping his face straight. 'To *not* investigate.'

I couldn't hide my guilty smile either. 'Well, Chloé asked my mum, who asked me... and I just happened to know someone staying there. *Et voilá*. Oh! And I also saw' – I retreated to the living room and came back with the painting Gilles had given me – 'some of his work there.'

Beau's jaw dropped. 'Whoa! Is that an original?' He jumped up and started examining the painting.

'Gilles de Vigan gave it to me at the party.'

'*Quoi*, are you having an affair or something? This is a *very* expensive gift. I mean, he must *really* like you.'

I bit my lip. I never told Beau about what happened between me and Gilles. I'd never told anyone. But I also hadn't expected Gilles to start giving me valuable artworks.

'It's gorgeous. Look at the way he's portrayed the tree there. That's not exactly where it is in real life, see? It should be over here, but that's outside the frame, so he altered the composition to make it look more interesting.'

Be that as it may, I still didn't like it. 'Do you want it?'

He gaped at me. 'Are you serious?'

'I don't particularly like it...'

'But it's a Piguemal!'

I shrugged and wrinkled my nose, but Beau's eyes started to sparkle.

'Have it. It's worth more to you than it is to me, no matter what it cost.' And Gilles was not in a position to complain about it. If he ever found out in the first place. 'But then, when you do leave, you'll have to take this place with you,' I added with a wink that I hoped would hide my anxiety about the subject.

He didn't pick up on it, as he was still studying the painting. 'Thanks, but two nights at my mum's was enough to make me want to escape again. I'm happy to be back.' He looked up. 'But are you sure? That's a lot of money you're giving me.'

His concern stirred me into a wide smile. 'No, *mon ami*, it's a painting of my house that you like and I don't. It would only be money if you sold it, and I know you wouldn't do that unless you had profound reasons to do so. Just enjoy all its weird angles and out-of-place trees.'

Forgetting to thank me, he smiled open-mouthed at the artwork, stroking its frame.

'I liked the one I saw at the Centre, though,' I said. 'Kids playing on a beach. That was a much gentler picture.'

Without looking up from the painting in front of him, Beau nodded. 'Must have been one of his earlier ones. He was doing all right with them, but he only became famous when he started putting more of an edge in his pictures, like this one.

Incredible that he chose your house to paint. He was based in the Auvergne but travelled around, like he must have done for that beach scene too.'

With a little satisfied sigh, he finally put down the picture and got up to get a beer from my fridge.

I reached out and pulled the frame towards me. Yes, it was my house, but it also wasn't. Even the parasol by the pool was more grey than its actual cream colour.

'No!' Flailing my arms, I shooed Thibault away from the edge of the wooden table he was about to use to open the bottle. 'Use a bottle opener, like normal people. I don't want dents in my table.'

Exaggerating all his movements, he took the two steps to a drawer, opened it fully, and rummaged inside with ridiculous, confused sounds.

'It's on the hook, where it always is.'

He raised his eyebrows at me. 'You have a bottle opener?'

But his words hardly registered any more. I stared at the painting in my hands. 'Beau... when did this guy die?'

'Oh!' His eyes lit up as he pointed the unopened bottle at me. 'Nobody knows. It's one of those weird moments in art history. There was a decline in interest in Piguemal's paintings, and suddenly, he disappears! Prices shot up, and everyone expected him to make a remarkable reappearance, but he was gone. Presumed dead, so of course, his work got even more valuable. Every now and then a new one shows up, but he made his last painting in the early two thousands.'

I winced. 'Then I'm so sorry, but... this is a fake.' His face fell, and I continued, 'This is my parasol. Aunt Geraldine never had a parasol like that. This painting can't be more than a year old.'

He sank down on a chair, staring at the picture.

'If it makes you feel any better, it fooled Gilles too, and he's an expert.'

'It doesn't.' His gloomy voice reflected his expression, but after a few seconds, he straightened a little. 'Actually, it does. It's still an amazing picture, made even better because of its subject. I think knowing it is in fact your house in the picture, and not Aunt Geraldine's, makes it more attractive to me.'

His brave face touched me even more than his gratefulness had done. The lump in my throat only allowed me to nod, so I stood up to get him the bottle opener.

'How about, instead of butting into police investigations, we try to find out who painted this?'

He gave me a sideways glance. 'Catch a forger instead of a killer? Makes a change.'

I shrugged.

'I guess we could try...' He cast one last melancholy look at the painting, then put it to the side. 'Where do we start?'

'I'll ask Gilles where he got the painting. You find out about those new Piguemals that have been found. Where did they come from, how many were there, that sort of thing. Oh.' I frowned. 'We do have a shoot tomorrow, remember?'

'Yeah, but it's in the afternoon.' He was already scrolling on his phone, sipping his beer. 'It's only ten.'

Right. I must be the only tired one, then. I couldn't wait to hear Léon's soothing voice after all that had happened. He always knew exactly the right thing to say. Or maybe it was just because he said it that it calmed me down. But Léon hadn't called yet, and apparently, I had research to do. Reaching for the door to get my laptop, I suddenly turned.

'Hey! If you didn't know I had a bottle opener, how have you been opening your beers?!'

14

You're kind of my hero

I awoke with a scream, still feeling Franck's hands on my neck. I swallowed, wiping the sweat from my brow. As much as I tried to be brave during the day, he still got to me at night sometimes. I should have known, after what happened last night, that he'd be there in my nightmares. My first instinct was to go and check on Beau, but it was still dark out and he probably needed his sleep.

My watch told me it was only six, but I was wide awake. Even if I'd felt sleepy still, I wouldn't want to risk giving Franck more time in my brain. I showered and dressed, and by the time Thibault came stumbling down the spiral staircase, I'd already done a few good hours of photo editing. I'd also had to reassure half the village that Beau was fine.

'Morning, *marmotte*,' I sang, making him jump. 'Sleep well?'

Rubbing his eye with the palm of his hand, he stood against the early morning sunlight streaming in through the glass wall in the back of the studio. 'Coffee?' was the only thing he could manage.

I grinned like a proud mother, feeling far too happy to have him back here in one piece. 'I'll make you some fresh. I should take a break anyway.'

While we strolled across the courtyard to the main house, his brain turned on. 'Why are you in the studio so early?'

'I just had to be near you, *chéri*. That's normal for you, right?'

A grunt was all I got. Before coffee, his snark was always off. Something I took advantage of to no end. He made sure to get back at me throughout the day, so the equilibrium remained intact. As soon as the pot was on the stove, I picked up my phone. I'd sent Gilles a message earlier, but since I'd no idea what time he rose, I'd left the phone in the house.

'Surprise, surprise, Gilles got the painting from Galerie Grosse.'

Beau narrowed his eyes and raised his eyebrows, making me sigh and pour him coffee first. While Monsieur Fouquet woke himself up, I went through the messages. Gilles never sent one-line texts. He regarded it as bad manners not to write the equivalent of a letter back. I had to find the info I needed in between all his lectures about the local influences that had obviously played a part in the production of this painting, as

well as the evolved style forming subtle discrepancies in the...
He was making me yawn.

'I'm hungry.'

Oh good, Beau was ready to talk. 'Apparently, my painting was one of those ones found later. It should have a label on the back from a gallery up north that was supposed to have sold it twenty years ago.' I looked up at the coffee-sipping blondness. 'Obviously also a fake. Xavier must not have done his due diligence. Or maybe the gallery doesn't exist any more. That would have been a smart move by our faker. Shame we can't ask Xavier about it, but maybe his secretary will know more. Are you... up to it?'

I didn't want to address the issue directly, in case it would hurt his pride. If it had been me they'd shot at, I'd be shaking in a corner of my closet, refusing to open the door until they'd caught whoever did it. Thibault was made of sterner stuff, but if it was true what he said – that he didn't know who did it – he must be at least a little worried.

Beau took a deep breath. 'I'm not going to stay home and wait for the police to find a lead. I've... err...' His jaw muscles clenched before he continued, 'I've let my dad know. In this case, I think I trust my own network to come up with results more quickly.'

Talk about hurting his pride. I hated that I was part of the reason for the rift between Thibault and his dad, who had taken Franck's side, but I was so proud of my young friend, both then for standing up for what he believed was right, and now for swallowing his pride and reaching out. If he had half his son's decency, Thibault's father wouldn't hesitate to come to his aid.

Not really knowing how to express those feelings, though, I bent down for a quick hug and laid out my plans for the day. 'All right, then let's pay a visit to the gallery. We'll just... be careful. They're bound to know *something* we don't already know.'

'Fine. Can we have breakfast now?'

Thibault had been unusually quiet this morning. Though that was understandable given what had happened, I couldn't help feeling I was partly to blame. That nightmare about Franck hadn't helped either. Whenever I dreamed about him, I felt less sure of myself, his belittling remarks no less impactful then when he'd made them in real life. As we pulled into the parking lot behind the gallery, I bit my lip. 'I'm sorry.'

He looked up, raising his eyebrows. 'For what?'

'I don't know. It feels like the whole shooting thing is because of me. I know it's because of me. I don't want you to get hurt, but now I'm dragging you back to town, even though I have no way of protecting you, so we should probably just go back, and—'

'Julie.' He turned in his seat and I winced.

'Don't tell me it's not my fault. It is my fault. If I hadn't—'

'It's not!'

I bit my quivering lip again. The only time he'd raised his voice at me was two days ago, when he left to model for Jessica. Was he leaving now?

But instead of opening the car door, he rested his head against the seat. 'It would have been much worse if you'd stayed and done his bidding. You did the right thing. Franck's just a...' He searched for a word that would appear in my vocabulary, but apparently found nothing suitable. 'Every bad thing that's happened has been *his* fault. He went to jail for what he did. Don't you dare let him make you feel bad about it. He did that before, remember?'

Through the tears welling in my eyes, I studied his face. The serious face that made him look so much older. 'You don't blame me?'

He grabbed his painting and opened the car door. 'Let's go inside. We're being watched.'

What? I frantically looked around the concrete and asphalt at the back of the two rows of shops and apartments but found no one. Had he made that up in order not to have to answer my question? I hurried after him, around the building and through the glass front door with a metal G for a handle, still checking my surroundings to no avail. The gallery had reopened, but all the art had been adorned with a black ribbon. Thibault had retreated all the way to the back, and I followed him into a little corridor that wasn't visible from the big window in the front. Once there, he wrapped me in a hug so tight I could hardly breathe.

'Of course I don't blame you. I know I'm going to regret telling you this, but you're kind of my hero. You stood up to Franck, giving me courage to do the same. That he hates us is not your fault, nor mine. We'll just have to deal with it.'

'You're going to need a clean shirt,' I squeaked against his shoulder as I cried my eyes out. In response, he only tugged my head closer. How could *I* be his hero? I felt like I'd done nothing but cry the past few days, not knowing what was going to happen or what to do about it when something did. But knowing I still had Beau's support gave me renewed courage to face whatever was coming.

'Are you all right?' A woman's voice made me jump.

'She recently lost a dear friend, and all the black...' Beau always had an answer ready, truth or not.

I loosened myself from his embrace, rummaging in my purse for a tissue, but fingers with purple nail varnish held one up for me. I gave the woman a watery smile and asked if she had a bathroom so I could freshen up. It happened to be right next to me, so while I went in to sigh at the state of my face, I could hear the conversation between Beau and the woman.

'I know how she feels.' Now I felt bad for the pain in her voice. Lying was never my first choice and I hated that it had reminded the poor woman of her own grief. 'You may have heard that the owner of this gallery was... forcefully taken from us.'

'Yes... Frankly, I was surprised you'd opened already.'

A slight pause. 'That was... not my decision. But it has been abnormally busy, which I suppose was the reason for opening.'

'Don't you, as the manager, have something to say about that?'

Oh, I could just picture the woman's slight blush and her demure smile. I'd seen it happen on enough women around Beau in the past six months.

'I'm only acting manager. Monsieur Grosse used to do a lot of the work himself, though he relied on me for the administrational side of things. This family member that inherited the gallery contacted me yesterday and told me to open up and sell as much as I could. "Have a sale or something", is what he said.'

Beau groaned sympathetically. 'So he doesn't know how to run a gallery?'

'He's not interested. Xav— Monsieur Grosse always wondered how he could have such admiration for these beautiful
pieces when his family were...'

'Swine?'

There was no answer, so I imagined the woman had agreed
with a gesture or a look. I'd finished making myself look pre-
sentable but was hesitant to go out. Thibault certainly didn't
need me for extracting information from a woman. I'd only be
in the way.

'Is she all right in there?'

That was my cue to reappear. With my fakest smile on, I
opened the door and came face to face with a woman in her
fifties, only slightly taller than me, which made her still a short
woman. Her make-up and black hair said 'professional', but
her red-and-purple glasses said 'artistic'. She frown-smiled her
concern at me, but Beau was ready for action.

'The reason we came in, actually, was to see you.'

'Oh?' Her eyebrows came up over the rim of her glasses.

'We were hoping you could tell us a little bit more about this
painting that was bought here.' He held up the brown paper
parcel that contained the fake Piguemal and unwrapped it.

'Ah yes, a Piguemal. Splendid work, don't you think?'

'Are you sure?' He held her gaze in an intense stare that
made her twitch.

'You don't like it?'

'Are you sure it's a Piguemal?'

'If we sold it to you, I'm sure it's a Piguemal. Monsieur Grosse was very meticulous in his research on provenance.' Her voice was confident, but her fingers played with the hem of her dark purple jacket.

'I'd like to see this research, if I may.' Beau's authoritarian act – his voice slightly lower, his expression bored with the stupidity of those around him, and his expectant posture – worked despite his youth. I couldn't help but admire it, and the woman didn't stand a chance.

'If you'd like to follow me to the office, I'll see what I can do.' She led us up the stairs, finding courage while she was ahead to add over her shoulder, 'But if Monsieur Grosse found any evidence of provenance, he would have included it in the bill of sale.'

'In that case, I'd like to see your copy. You do keep copies, don't you?'

'Of course.'

A familiar woman's voice came out of the shadows on the dimly lit landing. 'Yvonne—'

'Not now, Anaëlle.'

I automatically bonjoured Jessica's friend, but that did not work in my favour.

'It's all right, they know me.'

Yvonne held her ground. 'This does not concern you.'

'Yet. I'm taking over the gallery,' she added to me and Beau.

'That has not yet been decided.' Yvonne waved us through an open door. 'Please, step into the office and excuse me while I talk to this lady.'

While entering the office space and propping the painting up on the large mahogany desk, Beau covertly asked me, 'Who is she?'

'One of Jessica's friends,' I whispered back. 'Lives in the commune.'

He narrowed his eyes, then fell back into his persona. 'Excuse me. I don't have time for this. Let her stay, as long as she's not a distraction.'

Anaëlle tucked in her chin as she frowned. She was about to burst out to Beau, but somehow the expression on my face must have warned her, because she glanced my way and held her tongue.

Yvonne gave her one last warning glance but then closed the door. 'Have a seat.' She claimed the swivel chair on the other side of the desk and rattled her fingers over the keyboard while Beau sat down and I turned my chair slightly, so I could keep an eye on Anaëlle, who leaned against an antique sideboard displaying modern art, including two of Jessica's pieces – one torso and one spiky blob. 'You are Gilles de Vigan?'

'My grandfather,' Beau said before I could explain. 'I'm afraid he's one of those more interested in the feel of a work than its authenticity.'

Both women nodded – Yvonne understanding, Anaëlle rolling her eyes.

'May I ask, why do you doubt the authenticity?'

Again, Beau cut me off with a lie. 'Look at the signature. It's different. Yes, the techniques are similar to later works, and the signature is confidently made, but the style is off. It's almost too smoothly late Piguemal.'

He'd gone too far. There was no way she'd fall for that kind of vague explanation. I prepared myself to save the situation when Yvonne picked up the painting and studied it.

'Yes, I see what you mean. It—'

'Ha! Now do you believe me?' Anaëlle's triumphant voice intruded with a dissonance that made us all frown.

'Excuse me?' Beau said.

'Anaëlle...' Yvonne almost groaned. 'It's simply a late work. Look, it has the Galérie Colmar label right here. You know they're famous for introducing Piguemal to the art world.'

'Exactly. They represented his early works.'

Everyone was quiet at that. Thibault stared at Anaëlle over his shoulder. Anaëlle stared at Yvonne, who stared at her screen, and I tried to find out by staring at everyone what exactly was going on.

'What does that mean?' I asked Beau. I'd meant it to go under the radar, but since nobody was talking, it sounded as loud as if I'd shouted it.

'It means the painting's a fake.'

'But we knew that, didn't we?' I still didn't understand why everyone seemed so shocked.

'It means Xavier was selling fakes. Knowingly. He was too sharp to miss something like that.'

'But didn't we already know that too?'

This time my soft voice did go under the radar, because Anaëlle added loudly, 'And I'm pretty sure I know who painted this.' She folded her arms, looking at each of us in turn with a provocative smile.

'Oh yeah?' Yvonne's voice had lost most of its professionalism by now. This obviously wasn't the first time Anaëlle had accused Xavier of selling fakes, but it seemed to be the first time Yvonne had to admit she was right.

'I'll show you.' Anaëlle left the room and came back with another painting, similarly sized to the fake Piguemal. She set it on the desk, turning it towards the window, and Yvonne held the Piguemal next to it. Beau and I had to get up and round the desk to see what she meant, but whatever it was, I didn't see it. The Piguemal was a picture full of contrast between light and dark, angles and organic shapes, whereas this other picture was a much friendlier scene, a romantic picnic in the woods, sunlight shimmering through the leaves overhead. Though it reminded me of... something.

'Hm,' Beau said, voicing my thoughts. 'Who is Roméo Paris?'

'He's one of my neighbours in the commune. Well, he was. He was killed two days ago.'

Beau and I shared a look. We both would like to see Jacqueline explain away this connection. On the other hand, we'd first have to explain the connection. And though I was sure there was one, I'd no idea what exactly it was. Who would want to kill both the forger and the dealer of forgeries? Why not simply expose them?

'He was very good,' Beau remarked.

'Ah. Yes. But. You see these leaves dappled with sunlight around the picnic scene? Paris couldn't have passed this off as a Piguemal. Even early Piguemals showed that artistic fire, the heated energy of creation that is lacking from this work. In your painting, Paris has tried to recreate some of that strength, the gutsy strokes with which Piguemal breathed life into an otherwise static scene, but it misses the vulnerability, doesn't convey the expression of angst in the way they leap off the canvas of a real Piguemal.'

I peered at both paintings, trying to make out how those words would connect the fake Piguemal to the murdered painter's work. I must be missing something.

'But if he could do this' – Thibault indicated the Piguemal – 'why do this instead?'

'He hated the limelight.' Anaëlle waved her hand dramatically over her head. 'Maybe that was it?'

Beau pulled down the corners of his mouth. I agreed that didn't seem a very good explanation.

'Do you think we could have a look at his studio? Did he have a wife or someone with the key?'

Anaëlle shrugged. 'His daughter, I suppose. But... would you mind if I hang on to this?' She picked up the fake Piguemal.

'Anaëlle! No!' Stretching out her hand, Yvonne recoiled from Anaëlle, her eyes wide behind her colourful glasses. 'You'll ruin the reputation of this gallery. It won't be worth anything. Is that what you want?'

'I'll only ruin the reputation of your precious Xavier. The gallery will soon have a new owner, but if you play your cards right, it won't be under new management. Can I borrow the painting, or what?' She addressed me, making Beau raise his eyebrows. Somehow, she'd seen through him. Maybe it was his mascara-streaked shoulder. Or perhaps she simply addressed me because she knew me.

'I'm not sure how long it would be until you'd have to hand it over to the police in evidence of a double murder case,' I said, closely watching her reaction. She didn't seem to care much that two people in her vicinity had died recently. 'Do you still think Jessica is guilty?'

'I never thought Jessica was guilty.' She waved her dramatic hand again but gave no indication of caring any more about the deaths. 'I only wanted her to learn not to be so lackadaisical when it comes to men treating her badly. I mean, where did she find this new guy? Literally on the side of the road! She can pick the bad ones a mile away.'

'I thought Xavier handled your art too,' I said.

'Yes, because he was the only one around here worth dealing with. But he sold fakes just as easily as the quality artworks, and I think he didn't stop there. Once I have access to his files, I'll prove he was guilty of at least overvaluing, and probably money laundering too.'

'All right, that's enough.' Yvonne spread her arms to herd us out of the office. 'I won't have you accuse my former employer without any form of evidence, especially since he can no longer defend himself. I have a gallery to run – *legally* – so I'm afraid I'm going to have to ask you to leave. I'm sorry you think your Piguemal is a fake, but other than the opinion of a particularly biased person, I have found no evidence to sustain your claim. *Au revoir.*'

She clicked her heels down the stairs and left us with Anaëlle on the gloomy landing.

'Nasty business, these murders,' Beau remarked. 'Have you been questioned about them?'

'Me?' Wide-eyed, Anaëlle pressed her hand to her heart. 'Why? I have nothing to do with all that!' She huffed past us and retreated after Yvonne.

'Weren't we supposed to leave the murders to the police?' I asked, looking at Anaëlle's descending back.

'Only if they can do their job without us.'

I was ready to go down as well, but Beau stayed back. 'You coming?'

'I left my painting in there.'

'I'm sure you'll get it back later.'

He'd already opened the door. 'It's my painting. I want it back. She should have locked the door if she didn't want us in here. And if we happen to find something related to police business, we'll be sure to let them know.'

Before he could close the door on me, I slipped inside. 'This doesn't feel entirely legal,' I hissed.

'As long as you don't break anything, we've only entered.' He opened one of the drawers in the giant, antique desk, then closed it again without rummaging.

'So, what are we looking for?'

'We're not looking.' He opened another drawer, lifted a folder, and closed the drawer again.

I opened my mouth to say another unhelpful thing, but footsteps on the stairs sent my heart into overdrive. 'Someone's coming!' I whispered instead.

Beau immediately dove underneath the desk, leaving me standing in the middle of the room with nowhere to go, and the footsteps were already on the landing. At the last moment I flattened myself against the wall behind the door, hoping whoever would enter wasn't going to pay attention.

The door flung open and Yvonne entered, leaving the door ajar. If she turned around, I was in plain sight. As silently as I could, I reached for the door handle and opened the door wide, so it would hide me. Yvonne rounded the desk, opened a drawer, took out a manilla envelope, and left, closing the door behind her.

I sagged to the floor in a puddle of melted nerves. 'Why do you do this to me?' I whisper-shouted at Beau, who resumed his search calm as could be. 'We weren't supposed to snoop.'

'I'm not snooping in Jacqueline's case. I'm trying to clear Jessica from that other detective's suspicion.'

I'd made my way around the desk, pushing the mouse to wake up the computer. 'Found anything, then? This is locked.'

'Not really, though it would have been suspicious if I'd found anything with a cursory glance that the police would have overlooked in their search of the place.'

I felt sick. I hadn't realised this was where a man was murdered two days ago. My gaze fell on the spiky blob on the sideboard. It couldn't be…

'But then, this is a different room, of course. Let's check the other office.' Beau strode past me to the door.

'Wait. You mean this isn't…?'

'Of course not. This room faces the front. You said Jessica escaped out the back.'

I hardly had time for a relieved sigh because Beau had already crossed the landing.

'Locked,' he mumbled while reaching for his back pocket.

Quickly closing the other door behind me, I made a strangled noise. 'Wouldn't that be the breaking part we're trying to avoid?'

He looked between the lock and his hand holding the set of lock picks he always carried. 'No one would know.'

'*I* would.'

He sighed. Putting his hand on my shoulder, he guided me downstairs. 'All right, we've been up here long enough. Let's go.'

I stopped at the bottom of the stairs, making Beau bump into me.

'Hey!'

'Ssh! Yvonne is right there. I forgot to ask her about the rings, but now she's talking to someone around the corner. Do you think I should interrupt? Like I said, we weren't supposed to snoop.'

'Would she even have noticed if Xavier's rings were missing? I say we keep this nugget to ourselves for now. Until we're sure Jacqueline can't accuse us of butting in, *non*?'

Nodding, I convinced myself I was happy with that answer so I didn't have to be rude to Yvonne. We were hunting an art forger, that was all. I would only mention the rings if Jessica was arrested.

We left the gallery and hurried around the building, still checking our surroundings for threats before turning a corner. My heart was in my throat by the time we reached the car. There was a note underneath the windscreen wiper, which Beau reached for. He read it, then crumpled it and put it in his back pocket.

'What does it say?' I was surprised I produced any sound at all, dry as my throat and mouth were.

'Done,' he said, avoiding my eyes as he got in the car. 'Taken care of.'

15

I have a favour to ask

Was Jessica ever going to get a chance to kiss him? After their almost-kiss the day before, every time she found herself alone with Alain, something got in the way. When Julie left, the police came. When the police left, Anaëlle was still there. When she finally left, it was time for dinner, but Jessica was out of food so they'd headed for the café in Saint-Maurice. Jessica had hoped for a hint of romance, but Alain didn't seem all that interested any more, so when she saw Julie, Jessica had waved her over. Then the whole thing with Thibault had happened, and by the time they came home, Jessica had gone straight to bed.

Alain had stayed, on the couch. Again. She hadn't even asked if he wanted to, but she figured he could always call a taxi. He hadn't. And then, this morning, he hadn't spoken more than a few sentences to her, though he stood closer to her than she'd consider casual. But they'd simply gone back to working. She concentrated on her sculpting, while he was on the couch with his laptop being a total distraction.

Suddenly, Alain closed the laptop and sighed. 'I... have a favour to ask.'

Jessica turned around to look at him.

He leaned back on the couch with his hands folded behind his head, his black shirt stretching over his chest. 'I know it's cheeky to ask you for anything since you're already giving me a place to stay...'

'What?' she asked when he didn't continue.

'Also, it's... kind of an odd request.'

Intriguing.

'Especially considering your history with the business.'

Doubly intriguing. Jessica put down the chunk of clay she was working with and gave him her full attention. What business did she have a history with that he could have an interest in?

'I did some work for Galerie Grosse. Built them a little thing that... Never mind. The thing is...' He licked his lips and put his elbows on his knees, gesticulating with his hands before he actually started explaining. 'You know I want to set up a new company, right? That's because... the old one was in my ex-girlfriend's name. Tax purposes and all that. I thought it was a good idea at the time. So now I'm supposed to pick up some papers, but they're expecting a woman. Also, they weren't very happy with the work I did, so...'

'You want me to pick up some papers from Xavier's? You do realise they know me, right? They may well think I killed him.'

Alain swatted his hand through the air as if discarding the whole idea. 'I know, I know. It's stupid. I mean, I can disguise myself and make up some story, but it'd be easier coming from a woman. Just forget it.'

'You'd wear a disguise just to pick up some papers?'

He snorted and glanced at her from under his eyebrows. 'They *really* don't like me. But a disguise doesn't have to be a full beard and shades, you know. As long as you don't look like they expect you to. If I go in looking like a buyer of expensive art, they won't associate me with that builder from a few months ago. But you wouldn't need a disguise. You could walk right in, and if they're hostile, you go, "Relax, I'm only here for the papers for Shish-Kebab." You'd just confirm their bad impression of you. They wouldn't think twice.'

'The papers for what?'

He rolled his eyes. 'The company's name was Shish-Kebab. Don't ask.'

Jessica chuckled. A construction company called Shish-Kebab. Or, was it even construction? He'd told Julie he found struggling companies to help. But Galerie Grosse had never struggled. Oh, but he'd 'built' them something, of course.

'Do you think I could do it?' Suddenly, she was intrigued to see if she could pull it off. She hadn't actually been inside the building all that much. Most of Xavier's events had been for buyers, and if they went out together, she never came to the gallery. He would always meet her at whatever venue he'd picked. Looking back on their relationship, she still couldn't believe she'd let him make all those decisions for her. Now that he was gone, would his personnel have come to the same conclusion? Although, of course, he was their boss, and he was supposed to make the decisions, she was almost sure he had influenced their opinions on people and things. But perhaps there was still a chance she'd find someone on her side.

'I'm sure you could. But I thought you didn't want to? In fact, I don't think it's actually a good idea. Forget I asked.'

Though she was 95 per cent sure he was playing her, he was being so obvious about it that she didn't really mind. Besides, what harm could it do?

'I'll go wash my hands.'

'Are you sure?' he called after her as she disappeared into the kitchen.

'*Pas de soucis!*' she called back. In her mind, she was already going through what she would say to the gallery attendant, but when she turned around for the towel, she bumped into Alain.

'Thanks,' he said softly while he cupped her cheek with his hand. 'Just one more favour, though?'

As Jessica smiled up at him, she crossed her fingers that Anaëlle would stay away this time.

The door remained firmly closed.

Thirty minutes later, Jessica took a deep breath and pushed open the black-ribboned glass door. Though she was still a bit apprehensive about what kind of welcome she'd get, the pleasure of helping Alain outweighed her uneasiness. Thinking about him brought a glow to her cheeks. How could Anaëlle and Julie not see how amazing he was? But then, they hadn't kissed him. If they had, maybe they wouldn't be able to stop smiling either.

It was busy in the gallery. Several people were casting their critical looks over her spiky blobs. These, at least, were the real thing, she noticed when she passed them looking for someone she recognised. That woman with the red-and-purple glasses, she looked familiar.

'Excuse me,' Jessica said in the appropriate hushed tones, 'I'm here for the Shish-Kebab paperwork?'

The woman looked her up and down. 'You're Jessica Rose, aren't you?'

Jessica inclined her head in such a way that it could be a nod, but that she could still claim otherwise if the woman was going to show her the door.

But the woman sighed. 'I suppose so. One less thing to worry about.' She told Jessica to wait and disappeared upstairs.

Those papers were a worry? A niggle of doubt made Jessica's palms itch. It was probably just a figure of speech, though. With Xavier gone, his underlings would have a mountain of things to go through and clear up.

The gallery employee returned with a manilla envelope with a woman's name on it.

That was easy. '*Merci.* Do you mind if I have a look around?'

Shrugging, the woman held out her hand in invitation. It was odd, but without the pressure of Xavier appearing at any moment, Jessica enjoyed looking at other people's art. All the pieces on display were post 1950, but other than that, they had nothing in common. Some were classically figurative, others abstract. Most of it was serious, but some pieces were silly. There were sculptures in clay and glass, paintings, and even textile works that begged to be touched, though Jessica knew better than to try.

When she'd almost completed her relaxed amble around the space, a woman came strutting into the gallery on red patent leather stilettos and a shoulder bag to match. She didn't bother with any of the art but immediately strode up to the gallery attendant, who had been tapping away on a tablet. Jessica was too far away to hear what was asked or answered, but the hissed reply was all too clear. 'What?! Who is she, and why does she have my invoice?'

Perhaps this would be a good time to leave. Though Jessica had no idea if those words had anything to do with her, she didn't intend to stay and find out. Back in her little friend the 2CV, though, she panted to remain calm and felt her forehead growing damp. What had her impulsiveness got her into now? A man she didn't know asked her to do a strange thing and she immediately agreed. All because she wanted a kiss. A really good kiss, but still. What was wrong with her? On the other hand, if taking those papers was illegal, would the gallery attendant have given her access? She knew who Jessica was and that her name wasn't on the envelope. So that must not have mattered. Right? If she asked Alain about it, would he give her a straight answer?

A memory surfaced, and Jessica's head whipped round to the entrance of the gallery. That voice! Was that...? She tried to remember the voice of the woman who'd had the undocumented appointment with Xavier after her. But the more she tried to remember, the less sure she was it was the same voice she'd heard.

She started her car and drove off, still trying to work out whether she'd heard the voice before and if she was now morally obligated to return to the gallery and accuse that woman of... something. Her friend turned into the supermarket parking lot. Why had it brought her here? Well, as long as she was here, she might as well get some groceries. She had the feeling she was out of... some things. Maybe get a trolley.

When she arrived back at her studio, she parked her friend next to Anaëlle's car. Was she here *again*? That wasn't like her. Weeks could go by between sightings, and here she was two days in a row? Something was off. Something to do with the papers lying next to her on the passenger seat?

Jessica took a deep breath. Only one way to find out. She grabbed her grocery bag and exited the car, dumping the bag on the counter once she was inside.

'Jessica, finally.' Anaëlle came storming into the kitchen from the studio. 'Get rid of that man. Now. I saw him climb into a window at the Centre de Prédiction. If that isn't proof of something shady going on, I don't know what is.'

Frowning at her friend, Jessica blinked several times before her brain caught up. 'That can't be. I had the car. You must have seen someone else.'

Anaëlle grabbed her by the shoulders. 'Jess, I'm telling you, he's up to something.'

Clutching the incriminating envelope, Jessica still didn't want to admit she might have made a hasty decision that turned out to be a mistake. But this was yet another strange thing on the list. 'And you're basing this on, what? You saw someone climb in a window? How can you be so sure it was Alain?'

'Because I admitted it.' Alain leaned against the door post to the studio, not in the least perturbed by Anaëlle's accusations. 'I took a taxi to see a business associate, but they wouldn't let me in, so I had my associate open a window. It's really not as sordid as it seems.'

Oh, how she wanted to believe the simple explanation. 'Could you not have met somewhere else?'

He shrugged. 'This was easier.'

'The way it was easier to have me pick this up?' She waved the envelope in front of him.

Something in his laid-back attitude changed. It was subtle, but she got the feeling her pushback wasn't part of his plan, whatever his plan was. That there was a plan, however, she could no longer deny to herself. Her lips already mourned the loss of his kisses, but for once, she would make the right decision when it came to men. 'I'll call you a taxi.'

Anaëlle put a hand on her shoulder that was probably meant for support, but she shook it off as it felt more victorious than anything.

'Jessica, come on,' Alain pleaded while Jessica plugged in her phone. It had run out of battery halfway through her grocery run and she'd had to shop from memory. No doubt she'd missed half her list.

'It was just a meeting. So I went in through the window instead of the door. That's just because of their ridiculous rules. I haven't done anything wrong.'

'You know what? I don't believe you. I wanted to, but now I see all kinds of cracks in your act.' Her phone beeped with a voicemail. 'Please get your things and leave.'

If he'd refused, she didn't know what she would have done, but after calculating his options, disguised with a sad, pleading look, he turned to gather his effects.

'Well done,' Anaëlle whispered. 'You have to stand up to bullies. Even the ones that are clever about it.'

Jessica wished she'd shut up. She called a taxi and then listened to her voicemail. As the message went on, her eyes widened and she gaped at Anaëlle, who spread her hands open in front of her and mouthed, 'What?'

Putting down her phone, Jessica whisper-shouted, 'It's mine! Xavier left the building to me. What am I going to tell Alain?'

Anaëlle's eyes widened as well. 'You tell him nothing. You want him out of your life, not more involved!'

'He's bound to find out, though.'

'It'll buy you some time, at least. Maybe if he finds out you're the new owner, he won't want to rent the building any more.'

Alain came into the kitchen once more, carrying his backpack. There was a small, pale greyish-purple stain on his thumb that distracted Jessica. 'Are you sure this is what you want?'

Jessica wasn't sure at all.

'She's sure.' Anaëlle stepped in front and cut off anything Jessica might have said. Any other day, Jessica would have pushed her aside and told her she could make her own decisions, but could she? She'd invited a strange man into her home and done his dirty work. Why was she still in doubt as to whether it was a good decision to throw him out? Shouldn't it be obvious? Maybe letting Anaëlle do the talking wasn't such a bad idea.

Alain left without another word, and Anaëlle picked up Jessica's phone. 'There, he's deleted. You're better off, believe me.' She put the phone down but let her eyebrows droop when she saw Jessica's face. 'I'm sorry,' she said softly. 'It may not feel like it, but you know I'm right. Hey, tell you what. Since you don't own a TV, want to come watch a movie at mine?'

Nodding numbly, Jessica grabbed her keys, leaving her phone to charge. She wouldn't need it anyway.

16

These are all Xavier's

'Just like that?' I couldn't believe it would be that easy.

Thibault shrugged. He never liked to waste many words talking about his family, unless it was to complain about his mother's motherliness.

'Your father can do that? They'll leave you alone?'

'I'm sure whoever shot at me paid for it, but I don't really care how, because, you know, they shot at me.'

'So now it's over?'

'Says so, doesn't it?'

I closed my mouth, as it had been hanging open since we found the note and we'd been on our way home for several minutes already. 'But... that means Franck was the reason they shot at you, right? How would your father feel about that?'

Beau rubbed his eyebrow. 'Not necessarily. My dad has influence outside of our family, *tu sais*. Quite a bit, actually. Unless he deigns to tell me, I'll probably never find out who and why. But as long as they don't do it again, I'm okay with that.'

The conversation was over, leaving me far from satisfied. If Thibault was protected, did that courtesy extend to me? Or did it mean whoever shot at Beau would go after me next? I didn't know whether to be relieved or worried.

'Time to test out your ramp,' Beau remarked as we pulled into my driveway.

It took me a moment to drag myself out of my inevitable worries and realise what he meant. This afternoon's client used a wheelchair, so we'd had to come up with some interesting new poses. One of those poses had me commission a wooden ramp from a woman in Villefranche on which we could park the chair. Using the fan, we could hopefully make it seem as though she was hurtling down a hill. I still wasn't sure the scene wouldn't feel like a terrifying accident instead of the intended whoops-a-daisy moment, but my client had loved the idea and was adamant it would make a great picture.

'What do *you* think of it?'

'What, the ramp?' He got out of the car and sauntered to the studio entrance. 'Depends.'

Very helpful.

'If her character comes through in the pictures, it'll be fine.'

That actually was helpful. My pictures almost always brought out the adventurous side of my clients' character. To agree to have my kind of pictures taken, they'd have to have that adventurous side in the first place, and Yolande, my client this afternoon, was just about the most confident woman in the world. Beau was right. She could pull off this picture without making it seem like she'd lost control.

Unfortunately, with that out of the way, my worries about being shot came back with a vengeance. I tried to shoo them away by turning the volume up on the radio and singing along at the top of my voice while I was cooking, but by the time Beau came down for lunch, my singing had died down to an occasional hum. We ate our lunch in unusual quiet, which said enough about Beau's state of mind. We even cut our *sieste* short, both of us too restless to sit still.

While he did the dishes, I started on my final rounds. Surrounded by the comfort of my equipment, in an environment where everything did what I told it to do, I finally felt the tension in my shoulders disappear. Adjusting a light here and a screen there, I got excited about this job once more. Capturing a woman's daring on film was both a challenge and a satisfying victory, even before I'd seen the end result. Because this job was about the experience, the confidence boost of the moment. The pictures were almost just a memento of the occasion.

And Yolande was ready for it. She came early, arriving at the same time as Maile and already cracking jokes. This woman had the sexiest smile I'd ever seen. Her features alone were nothing special, but with that flawless black skin surrounding a smile with perfect white teeth, the confidence she radiated was extremely attractive.

I especially loved the effect she had on Thibault. Whereas he would make a show of himself with a client who needed a bit more courage, around Yolande he was almost docile. She bossed him around, but since he didn't seem to mind, I let her.

'See, now this is the way to travel,' she declared when Beau lifted her out of the chair and onto the white leather couch where she'd pose. 'Can I hire you, *mon lapin?*'

I almost snorted. Ordinarily, it was Beau finding animal names for all the women around him, but this time he was the bunny. I wondered how he liked it, but I couldn't hear his muttered response. Yolande burst out laughing and I was left burning with curiosity over what that little wink he gave her meant.

Somewhere deep down, I wanted him to feel awkward about the way she treated him. That surprised me when I realised it. I didn't understand. The clients he flirted with always seemed to love it. Yolande hadn't said or done anything he didn't do himself, so why would I want him to feel bad about it?

I didn't have time to examine my uncomfortable feelings further as the shoot got underway. I had to focus on getting the right angle on the wheelchair, but Yolande had clearly given the matter some thought and started bossing *me* around, and by four o'clock, I'd laughed so much that I'd forgotten all about my odd pettiness. I glanced at the wall clock and pretended to sniff.

'Sweet almonds. Céline must be close. Let's get you back into your own clothes, Yolande, so you can enjoy the local delicacies.'

Beau retreated before I could catch his attention, so I sent him a quick text. *Commune later?* He reacted with a thumbs up, so I focussed on sending Yolande off with as positive an impression as I could give her. Every client brings her own complications, but with Yolande, it had been smooth sailing almost every step of the way. I wished all my clients were that easy.

After I'd seen both Yolande and Maile out, I sent Beau another text. *Coast is clear.* He came strolling down the stairs almost immediately.

'Cupcake?' I'd saved him a coffee-walnut one, but he grimaced. I was aching to ask him why he was avoiding Céline when yesterday evening everything seemed fine between them. But with the shooting, the murders, and the fake painting, this wasn't the moment to broach that subject. Instead, I mimed putting on a deerstalker and puffing on a pipe.

'Let's go hunt a forger.'

Shaking his head, Thibault let out a huff of a laugh and pushed me towards the door. 'Let's just hope someone will be there.'

Our plan was to visit the artists' commune and hopefully talk our way into the painter's studio. If not, we'd have to settle for interviewing the neighbours, but as long as there was anyone at home, I trusted Beau's shady skills to get us in.

The commune appeared to be deep in mourning. When I'd visited the ceramics market, there were always lots of colourful decorations everywhere – bunting and mirrored lanterns gently dancing in the breeze – but they'd all been taken down. Some of the windows showed black ribbons similar to the ones in the gallery that morning. Inside one workshop, a wild-haired woman had even painted a black band over her eyes, though I couldn't be sure she didn't always do that, of course.

I stopped walking. 'Let's go back to the car.'

Beau halted a few steps ahead of me. 'What? Why?'

'This was a bad idea. All these people are heartbroken because one of them has died. Not only that, *murdered*. We can't just barge in here accusing him of forgery!'

'Who's barging? All we're doing is—'

'Julie?' My retreat was foiled by Anaëlle Sandhomme, who once again completely ignored Thibault and spoke only to me.

'I thought I might see you here soon. I've been looking out for you. Come, I'll introduce you to the girls.'

She pushed past Beau, who owned it by extending his hand and declaring, *'Après vous.'*

Anaëlle led us to a small house with a large barn at the back, its yellow stone façade broken up by dark brown shutters, some open and some closed. All around the house and barn were clusters of potted plants, blooming exuberantly, and the heavy scent of an overflowing wisteria made my head swim. The happy colours were in sharp contrast to the expression of the older teenager who answered the door.

'Rosa, *des clients*,' Anaëlle lied. Or maybe she didn't. Maybe she did believe Beau's uncle had bought the painting. She didn't have any reason not to, did she? Sometimes I really hated the lies Beau told so easily. I couldn't keep those different stories straight in my head and was always afraid I'd say the wrong thing and be found out.

Rosa, her strawberry blond hair tied in a simple ponytail at her neck, stepped aside and let us in without saying a word. Another young woman, maybe one or two years older than Rosa, with cropped black hair and pretty, light blue eyes, joined us in the tiny, sparsely decorated living room, a solemn and I thought slightly hostile look on her face.

'Can we see the studio?' Anaëlle was already halfway through the back door. Beau and I quickly followed, not wanting to be left behind in the gloomy atmosphere of the Spartan house.

'It's those girls we saw crying on the bench when you came back from your walk,' Beau whispered before we caught up to Anaëlle.

My head snapped up, but I caught myself in time not to look back. 'So which is the daughter and which is the friend?'

'They're more than friends.'

'Best friends?'

'More like girlfriends.'

I frowned at him, hesitating at the door to the barn that had fallen shut after Anaëlle. 'How do you know?'

He spread his arms wide. 'Give me some credit!'

Huffing, I opened the studio door and entered. Rows upon rows of paintings lined the walls of the surprisingly light space, leaning against each other on the floor. We'd approached from the south, but the entire north side of the roof was made of glass panels that could be shuttered individually via an intricate system of levers on a panel in the corner, above a small desk. Not very high-tech, but effective. An easel stood in the middle of the barn, surrounded by tables laid with bizarre arrays of twigs and fruit, jugs, jars, and one herring that should have been cleared away long ago. I suppressed a gag and focussed on the sofa on the other side of the easel. A kimono had been discarded on it, which I supposed the sitter had worn, but it was accompanied by the taxidermied head of a stag and a little pile of silver jewellery.

'Ah!' Beau exclaimed. He'd been looking through the stacks of paintings on the far wall and now took one out that looked like a landscape. 'Piguemal. Right here in the corner. Extremely good one, too.'

Anaëlle hurried to his side and gasped softly. 'Are you sure that's not real?'

'Why would it be? Look around. To say this man was versatile would be an understatement. I think he could have successfully forged a whole range of painters, but all the other works are signed Roméo Paris. I wonder why he chose Piguemal.' He stared at the painting he held almost reverently in his hands.

Anaëlle for once had nothing detractive to say. She beheld the painting with a dreamy look of admiration.

'Do you paint?' I asked her.

That hardened her eyes. 'I dabble. Unfortunately, *my* art seems to be recognising other people's greatness. The creator in me will never measure up. No, that's not false modesty. I don't do crap like that. I say it like it is.' She didn't have to tell me. But I applauded her self-knowledge.

'In that case, can you tell us about Roméo Paris? Do you have any idea why he would fake Piguemals when he was clearly a good artist in his own right?'

'Skill and talent don't always guarantee fame,' she answered wistfully. Her shoulders sagged as she turned, glanced around, and then made for the sofa. I backtracked to face her but made sure I stayed well away from the disgusting fish.

'I've had to go over what I know about Roméo to the police already, of course,' Anaëlle started. 'But I didn't know about his forgeries. I would have said if I knew.' She sat up straighter with those words and said them loud and proud. 'Not speaking ill of the dead and all that nonsense, I don't go for it. I didn't like him and I said so.' She deflated again. 'But that was more because of how he treated Rosa. She was never allowed anything. You've seen the house. Paris never spent money on anything that wasn't absolutely essential. I thought he must not earn much with his art, but now that can't be true. He must have had money.'

She narrowed her eyes at the art surrounding her, then looked me in the eye. 'And he couldn't stand Tessa, even though he let her stay. The poor girls are devastated by his death. But I'm going to make sure they're taken care of. Don't you worry. They deserve a bit of happiness. Even if we have to unmask Roméo as a forger, I'll make sure none of it reflects on Rosa. We at the commune all love her dearly. She's such a caring child. Well, hardly a child any more, I suppose.' Her fingers played with the jewellery while she stared at a point between me and the table that held the fish.

Beau had been going through more of the paintings and came back with another canvas, this time of a headless model on the same sofa Anaëlle occupied. 'Here's another. Not a typical Piguemal subject, but nonetheless signed as such. Do you think these fakes had anything to do with his death?'

Her eyes bulging, Anaëlle took in a gulp of air as she clenched her fist around some of the jewellery and a slip of kimono. 'Do you think? Oh! Oh, and then... Then it makes sense that Xavier was involved. And... Oh, that's too horrible. But you're right. I hadn't thought. Unbelievable. How did I not see?' Her fingers relaxed around the armrest and she put a shaky hand to her brow. She groaned. 'Ohhh, and that's going to make everything so much more difficult with... I'm sorry, I have to make a call.'

She got up, but one of the rings had slipped around her finger and as she pulled it off, she gasped again. 'This is Xavier's!' Pouncing on the little pile of jewellery, she pulled out several other bulky rings. 'These are all Xavier's.' Her breath came in short bursts and her knees gave way, landing her uncomfortably hard on the concrete, paint-splattered floor. Both Beau and I jumped to her aid, Beau helping her up onto the sofa, and me trying to ease the rings from her clawing hands.

'That's not right!' she shrieked. 'Xavier is dead. Roméo is dead. They can't be here. They can't. It's not right.'

Thibault positioned himself between Anaëlle and my hand now holding the rings. I made sure to quickly pocket them as I took out my phone. No reception. Really? I shouldn't be surprised. There were plenty of valleys around here that were overlooked when it came to mobile phone reception, but most were so small that you only passed through them, or they held one or two houses at the most. I had not expected a whole commune living without mobile phones and grumbled about it internally as I scrambled to the main house in search of a landline.

Both girls were quietly sitting on the threadbare sofa, holding hands, when I came in. 'Can I use your phone, please?' I asked bluntly. We were intruding on a stranger's grief, and it made me feel like whatever I said or did was terribly rude.

'Over there.' Tessa pointed to a corner where an old-fashioned corded phone stood on its own tiny table. I had to kneel on the floorboards in order to operate it, making me pray to the gods of telecom for a connection to Jacqueline. Copying the number from my own phone, I turned away from the girls, although I'd avoided looking in their direction, so I didn't know if they were paying any attention to me.

'Gavel.'

'It's Julie. I'm at the artists' commune and—'

'Why?' If that wasn't a threat, I didn't know what was. But I had to tell her what we'd found.

'We weren't snooping! Not in your case, anyway. I got this painting and—'

'Why are you calling me?'

'You could be a little less exasperated. I'm only trying to help.' I knew she was busy, but I hadn't done anything wrong. 'We've found Xavier Grosse's rings.'

'On my way.'

'You're welcome,' I grumped at the already beeping line. Dusting off my skirt, I glanced at the girls. Rosa was still staring into nothingness, but Tessa had perked up.

'Grosse, isn't that the murdered art dealer?'

I nodded, thinking that information probably wasn't classified. When it came to Jacqueline and her eternal disappointment in me, I had developed a cautiousness that others reserved for state secrets.

'And you've found his rings... here?'

Oh. That might have been classified.

Rosa looked up at Tessa's agitation, questioning first her friend and then turning to me with eyes full of emotion. At first, I thought I saw fear, but it must have been a mix of sadness and confusion because she asked, 'Rings? Like, finger rings? Why would he take those off?'

'The question is, why are they here? If there's a connection, maybe Grosse's killer also got your dad.' Tessa rubbed circles on Rosa's back, but her eyes bored into mine. Jacqueline had better hurry. I would be a terrible spy. One angry look from the villain and I would spill all the secrets. Even the state ones.

Ten minutes later and I was still nailed to my spot by the back door. I was dying to know if Beau had found any more evidence, but what if that little bit of information was enough to make the girls flee? Why they would flee I'd no idea, but if they left while I wasn't paying attention and they turned out to be vital to the case, I'd never hear the end of it. Although, in those ten minutes, I'd already thought of every possible scenario in which the girls could be linked to the murders, but though they were obviously close to the painter and they knew of the art dealer at least, I couldn't see the connection to Chloé's assistant. Unless Beau was wrong and that had been an accident after all.

Finally, there was a knock on the door. Rosa winced, but Tessa squeezed her hand and got up to open the door.

'I'm sorry to bother you again, Tessa. How are things?' The humble size of the house allowed me to hear every word spoken at the front door all the way at the back. This was Jacqueline's understanding tone. The one that I seemed to hear less and less of these days. It wasn't my fault that I kept getting mixed up in her work. If anything, I needed her support more, now that Franck was roaming the streets again. But instead, she was giving it to these girls she hardly knew. Oh. Was I getting jealous?

Ashamed, I turned my gaze towards the window and studied the unassuming barn until Jacqueline had time for me. Unfortunately, the barn exterior was just about as boring as it could get, so I still got impatient. When Jacqueline finally came my way, I had to keep myself from sighing. Instead, I dug the rings out of my pocket and held them up.

'I guess we can forget about fingerprints?'

I was ready to scream. 'Anaëlle had already had them in her hands, so I didn't think it mattered any more. But next time, I'll keep new evidence to myself.'

'That would be against the law.'

'And hello to you too.' Quietly seething, I led her to the barn, where I left Beau to explain what had happened. He'd at least managed to calm Anaëlle down. She was now fidgeting with her nails, leaning against the desk in the corner near the window controls, where I joined her.

'Are you all right?'

'Yes, thanks, I'm fine now.' Though quieter than usual. 'I just can't believe I didn't see the connection. Someone must have found out Roméo was making forgeries and Xavier was selling them, and they killed them both. At least that clears Jessica.'

'Seems a bit extreme?' The forgeries made for an obvious connection, but I'd already discarded it for that reason. 'And how would that involve Wylène Chiche?'

'Who?'

'The girl who died at the Centre de Prédiction?'

Her blank face said enough. 'How is she connected?'

'Exactly,' I mumbled, but Anaëlle didn't press me for more. 'Do you think the girls will be all right?'

'Yes.' A sliver of her normal confidence shone through in that word. 'They'll only have to weather it for a few months before Rosa turns eighteen. Then she won't need anyone to make her decisions for her. I'm sure we can find someone to act as her guardian in the meantime. I'll do it myself if I have to. I know I'm not family, but honestly, she'll be better off than with him.'

'Was he... violent?'

'Oh, no!' She shook her head. 'We would have intervened if that were the case. She was simply never allowed any-thing. No sweets, hardly any new clothes, no going out... Friends never lasted long because she wasn't allowed to have them over or go to their houses. It's a miracle Tessa found her way in somehow. I'm sure it will take some time for Rosa to get over the shock, but it wouldn't surprise me if she'll bloom afterwards, when she finally gets to spend all that money he must have from selling the fakes.'

'Unless he had debts? Like from gambling?' I wasn't snooping. This was genuine interest.

Snorting, Anaëlle looked at me down her nose. 'The only thing he ever did was paint. He came here when Rosa was little more than a baby, and she was practically raised by the rest of the village. No, he had that money somewhere, and now she'll get to enjoy it.' A proud smile graced her face, making me wonder if 'the rest of the village' meant mostly her. How far would she have gone to free a girl she saw as her daughter?

I glanced at Jacqueline, who was still interrogating Thibault. Should I inform her of my thoughts, or would that only be considered 'butting in'? Probably best to keep quiet for now and see where her investigation led her.

My gaze drifted around the room, taking in all the different styles of painting and all the different subjects. Difficult to market, I would imagine. Was he a colourful expressionist or a meticulous realist with a penchant for chiaroscuro? I saw evidence of both, and every style in between. The desk I was leaning against had a drawer. Would he keep some of his sales records here?

Careful not to make any noise, I slowly slid open the drawer, but the only thing in there was a photograph that I took out and examined. A greyish-blond man hugged a girl of about ten years old. Since the girl was clearly Rosa, the man must be Roméo Paris.

'They seem happy enough,' I remarked when I realised Anaëlle was looking over my shoulder.

'Of course. They were all the family the other had, so they made it work. There were plenty of moments like that too. They did love each other. But I still think it'll be good for Rosa to come out of this isolation.'

I traced the lines of Roméo's face, in my head criticising the lighting of the picture. 'He was quite a bit older, wasn't he? Do you know what happened to her mother?'

Anaëlle shrugged. Whether she didn't know or didn't care, she wasn't going to tell me.

'What's that?' Jacqueline pointed her chin at the photograph in my hands.

'Just a picture of Rosa and her dad.'

Apparently, she couldn't find a reason to reprimand me over that, because she stared at the floor when addressing me. 'So you found out that Paris was a forger. That's... good work. We had no idea.' She said it quickly, as if giving compliments physically hurt, but I revelled in her words nonetheless. 'But I thought I told you to stay out of this,' she couldn't help adding.

'I'm not involved. Beau must have told you how we were tracking down my painting and we just happened—'

'I thought it was his uncle's.' Anaëlle glared at me.

See? This is why I shouldn't lie! My mouth opened and closed as my cheeks heated up, but Jacqueline saved me from having to answer.

'I need to go see if Marc has found out anything from the girls and then I'll have to inform Chagrin that I have new evidence in his case. I'm sure he'll be delighted.' Was that sarcasm? I honestly couldn't tell. 'Julie, I suggest you find something else to occupy yourself with, now that you know... you know. And next time, tell me up front if you're going anywhere near any of my cases. Yes, yes, you couldn't have known about the rings.' She held her hand up when I opened my mouth. 'But you knew the circumstances. You're not an idiot.'

She turned and exited the barn, leaving me yet again with burning cheeks. 'Let's go,' I barked at Beau as I stalked past him.

He raised his eyebrows, but dutifully followed me to the car, where I got in the passenger's seat and crossed my arms. Did I look like a toddler having a tantrum? Probably, but I didn't care. All this time I had purposely had nothing to do with any murders whatsoever, and still I got chided for getting involved. I had half a mind to get involved for real and show her. Had I not told her from the beginning to look out for those rings? Still, how they ended up in the studio of Roméo Paris, I had no clue, but right now, I was sure I could find out if I put my mind to it.

17

Who did it?

'Attendez!'

Beau had one leg in the car already but froze at Jacqueline's voice. She gestured for me to lower my window, which I did, but only halfway. Even in this mood I couldn't justify that level of pettiness, though, so I opened the window fully while Jacqueline started her version of an apology.

'I've been crazy busy with these murders. My boss wants me to write Wylène Chiche's death off as an accident, but I can't find any trace of the diet pills or the *grattons* in her room. Your fake painting and these rings are the first real clue I've had in Roméo's death. I thought I was going to have to charge those girls, as he didn't seem to be in contact with anyone else, but you've proved a link between his case and the art dealer's, for which your friend is still the main suspect, by the way.'

How to react... 'You're welcome' was the standard passive-aggressive answer, of course, but not very original. 'Happy to help' was too big of a lie. 'Apology accepted' felt gracious to me but would probably come out blunt.

My desire to help won out. 'You don't think they're all connected? Wylène was at Galerie Grosse the day before.'

Jacqueline sighed. 'I know. Perhaps, now that I have concrete evidence to connect our cases, Étienne will be a bit more forthcoming in sharing case notes. He thinks I'm an overachiever.'

'He's not completely useless as a detective, then.' I regretted the words, true as they were, instantly.

Jacqueline straightened and took her hand off the car. 'Have a safe trip home.'

Beau got in and grinned at me. 'You had to be curious, didn't you.'

'I was trying to help!'

'*Sans doute.*' Meaning he in fact doubted it very much.

If my arms hadn't been crossed already, I would have crossed them. Instead, I squeezed them a little bit tighter and sulked all the way back home.

That's when Beau announced, 'I know who did it.'

'How?' There was no way he'd figured it out before me. Even though I'd purposely not thought about anything connected to any of the murders because I'd promised my ungrateful police friend. 'Who?'

Instead of answering, Beau got out of the car and ambled to the front door. 'Is it time for dinner yet?'

'It's only six. Who did it?'

He opened a cupboard, took out a cured sausage, juggled a knife out of the block – I hated when he did that – and took a seat at the kitchen table, cutting up the sausage and chewing lazily while I glared at him, my knuckles white around the purse I was supposed to have put down on the table.

'Richard Othman.'

'The guru guy at the Centre?' My fingers relaxed and I sat down across from him. 'Why?'

'He's the only one possibly connected to all three victims.'

'Possibly.'

He waved a slice of sausage through the air. 'You said you'd seen a Piguemal at the Centre. It could be a fake.'

I gasped. I actually gasped. That possibility hadn't occurred to me yet. At all. Suddenly, all kinds of ideas I should have had long ago came flooding into my brain, and I had to fetch a notepad from the living room to get them all down.

'So, you think it's Othman.' I put his name at the top of the paper with three lines radiating down. At the first, I put Wylène Chiche. 'She was a guest in his venue, which makes for a link between them. But. Would he be so stupid as to murder someone in his own exclusive facility and risk its reputation?'

He shrugged. 'Murderers aren't all geniuses.'

Évidemment, I conceded. Still, it would be a huge risk for Othman. I wrote Xavier Grosse at the middle line. 'They were friends. Good friends. When I talked to him, he was genuinely upset that he'd lost an important person in his life.'

'Yes, but maybe he'd already lost Xavier as a friend because of something Xavier did, like sell him fake paintings, and that's why he killed him.'

'That's quite a big maybe. So what about Roméo Paris?'

'He obviously painted the fake.'

I tapped my pen on Roméo's name. 'In that case, we'll first have to make sure the painting in the Centre is actually a fake. Because if it's a real Piguemal, your theory falls to pieces.' I bit my lip. 'But there's more. Why were Xavier's rings in Roméo's studio and how did they get there?'

'How is obvious: the killer left them there.'

'All right, but why?'

He swallowed. 'To throw us off the scent? To confuse us? To get rid of them?'

'Ooh! Could there be an unexpected accomplice, like in Montmales?'

He raised both eyebrows at me, and I slumped in my seat. Talk about far-fetched. But Xavier's rings turning up at another murder victim's house just didn't make sense. We'd only found out about the link between Xavier and Roméo that morning. Why would the killer point us to a link he couldn't have known we'd already discovered? Wouldn't it have been better for him if we didn't know the two were connected?

But then, everyone knew Roméo sold his paintings through Xavier, so the link wasn't exactly obscure to begin with.

'But why take the rings in the first place?' Beau frowned at the sausage in his hand.

'I think I know the answer to that. I think the killer meant to be seen driving Xavier's car away from the gallery, as indeed he was, by Jessica. She said she recognised him by his rings. Only, the killer didn't count on Yvonne, the secretary, to find Xavier so quickly. I think they wanted everyone to think Xavier had been killed later, which means they probably have an alibi for later. It can't have been too soon after, though, since they still had to hide the car.'

'So we need to find out where Othman was that morning.'

'And who the client was that Xavier met with after he spoke to Jessica. They had a window of about half an hour, which would be more than enough to murder someone.'

Beau cut another slice of sausage. 'Or to have a quick meeting and leave with plenty of time for the real killer to show up.'

'Perhaps, but I'd still like to know who it was.'

'*Bien sûr*, you always want to know everything.'

'I have to, if I'm going to solve this murder.'

'Are you, though?' He looked me in the eye, his expression intense. I knew what he meant. I'd said I wouldn't get involved. None of it had anything to do with me. If I was going to investigate, it would be out of pure curiosity. Okay, and a little out of spite. Maybe a bit more than a little out of spite.

I sighed, ready to give up.

'No, I'm asking you,' Beau said. 'Will you solve these murders? For Wylène. For me?'

Oh. I stared at him, my mouth open. From his confidence in me alone, my heart bloomed. But it also bled at his motivation. Underneath all that cockiness, he wasn't too proud to ask for help – for a girl that had been taken before he'd had a chance to get to know her.

I swallowed the lump in my throat while I took out my phone. 'I'll ask Chloé if she can get us into the Centre de Prédiction. She seemed to have some clout with Othman.' Putting the phone down after hitting send, I looked at Thibault. 'But we'd better be prepared. This' – I gestured at the paper with the four names on it – 'isn't going to cut it. We need at least one good theory.'

Beau's face brightened until it practically shone. 'Ah!' he said, taking my hand and dragging me out across the courtyard and to his room above my studio. There, he pulled a board-room-sized drawing pad from behind the sofa and flipped page after page over the top. When he put it flat on the coffee table, he'd uncovered a page without sketches, filled with scribbles and arrows in different colours.

Wide-eyed, all I could say was, 'Wow.'

'So, on this side, I have all the people involved and where they were on Tuesday, as far as I know. Here are all the possible motives.'

'And I suppose this knot of arrows shows how they're all related?'

'Oui!' His beaming face made me laugh.

'And the conclusion of all this is that Richard Othman is a killer.'

At that, his smile faltered. 'Well... He's the most likely candidate. But apart from that, I have no proof.'

'All right. Another thing that I've just noticed...' I pointed at the middle of his suspects list. 'Why is Moira on there? She's only here to have her picture taken with Marie and the others. By me, not unimportantly! She's my client.'

'Being your client doesn't automatically exclude anyone from being a killer.'

I gave him a mock scowl. 'I think it does. But explain.'

'It's actually only because she's at the Centre and we know her,' he admitted. 'There's a line to Wylène because you said she'd talked to her, but other than that, I don't see any connection.'

'Okay. Points for thoroughness.' I patted his shoulder in the most patronising way, but he let it slide. Sinking to my knees, I started to really study his work. After a while, I had to admit he seemed to have done a good job of it. 'You're right. Tessa and

Rosa might have been good candidates for Roméo's murder, but although they knew Xavier, they had nothing to do with Wylène. Jessica would have been a good suspect for Xavier, but though she knew Roméo, again, she had nothing to do with Wylène.' I turned my head towards Beau, who was doodling on the couch. 'And also I just don't believe she could murder anyone.'

He shrugged, not looking up from his drawing. '*Nan*, neither do I, but she's involved, so she's on there.'

'Alain...' I considered the next name on the list. 'Do we know anything about him at all?'

Still keeping his eyes on his drawing, Beau said, 'Millionaire.'

'What?!'

'Google him.'

I fumbled for my phone, getting more and more frustrated because it was in my pocket in one of the many folds of my skirt and it seemed determined to stay hidden. By the time I'd tapped Alain Coquard's name into the search engine, my breath was coming in short bursts. Rows of photos of the handsome man on red carpets in expensive suits, a different gorgeous woman on his arm in each of the pictures. He had his own Wikipedia page, explaining how he'd made a fortune in high street fashion.

'Does Jessica know? She must have looked him up before she decided to take him in.'

'I don't think she did. From what she said about it, she seems to think she's doing a good deed.' He looked up then and grinned in that I'm-going-to-make-a-dirty-joke way, so I held up my finger.

'Don't.' I glanced at my phone again. 'We should probably talk to them again as well. Do you think he could be a murderer? Maybe we should just go there right now…'

The most horrific scenes started playing in my head in which Alain was brutally slaying Jessica with clay torsos, and I was already getting up when Beau said, 'Chill. I don't think he has anything to do with anything. Wrong place, wrong time sort of thing.'

'But why wouldn't he tell her who he is?'

'Does it matter?'

I was ready to say of course, but maybe Beau was right. If Jessica was willing to take in a stranger and help him, she could do that for a rich man just as well as for a poor one. Though why on earth anyone would let a strange man into their house and let him stay was beyond me.

Beau stretched out on Aunt Géraldine's old couch and folded his hands behind his head. 'I added Anaëlle later, because she knew both Xavier and Roméo, but again, no connection to Wylène.'

I tugged at a strand of hair from my ponytail. 'Maybe we're coming at this from the wrong angle. If you want to solve

Wylène's murder, we have to start with her. What do we know about her?'

'Not much. I know what she liked, but she didn't tell me anything about her family or where she came from. She was excited about her job, but she mainly talked about everything Chloé did. And then it was mostly about the way she did things, because by the end, I still had no idea what business she was actually in. I tried looking Wylène up online, but every mention is only in relation to Chloé Walkure.'

'And what is it she does?'

'High-end property. Business buildings and the like. Hotels as well, I think. Wylène said it was a global conglomerate that Chloé had worked really hard for, but then she segued into art again, how they always liked to hire local artists for their buildings.'

'Do you think that could be a connection between her and Roméo? Moira did say... Oh, what was it? Moira had bought a painting for her dad in Jarnioux... and Wylène said it reminded her of the painting she'd bought from Xavier. Sooo...'

'You think she bought a fake Piguemal? But Piguemal wasn't local.'

'Was she the type of person who would know that? Some people appreciate art without really knowing anything about it. Xavier could have told her any old lie.'

He thought about that. 'No, I think she'd have seen through that. She didn't mention Piguemal by name, but she knew loads of others. And I mean, your painting fooled me too.'

I hid a smile at his implied expertise, but he certainly knew more than I did. 'We need to see the painting she bought. But something has been bothering me... Wylène ate *grattons* with diet pills, which could easily have been seen as an accident. According to Jacqueline, that's exactly what she's supposed to declare it was, even though she can't find the pills or the food.'

'Moira sneaked in some crisps, though, didn't she?'

'True... We'll have to find out how difficult that was.' Picturing Moira in her room at the Centre, I found another memory. 'I just thought of something. Anaëlle's mother is staying at the Centre. That actually connects her to all three as well.'

Beau frowned. 'It connects her to the Centre, though not necessarily to Wylène. But draw an arrow, anyway.' He threw me his pencil, and I added another line to the tangle.

I tapped the pencil against my lip. 'She's hoping to take over the gallery, and she feels strongly about Roméo and his daughter... If Wylène's death is not connected, she's in line for prime suspect. For the other two, I mean. But that still doesn't give us a clue about Wylène.'

'That's probably because the only one actually connected to Wylène, as far as we know, is Chloé.'

I shook my head. 'You should have seen her when she found out. She was completely distraught. Also, she's the one refusing to believe Wylène's death is an accident. Why would she do that if she could get away with it being an accident?'

'It also still leaves the other two. Although it could be coincidence that someone else killed them on exactly the same day.'

'Yes, Chloé doesn't have any links with Xavier or Paris, unless the painting she bought is a fake. But she was in a floatation tank when Xavier was killed. Same goes for Jessica, by the way. Even if we considered her a suspect, she was with the police in her own studio at the time the painter was murdered. None of these people really have a good motive, or the right opportunity, to kill all three victims. But if we look at them individually, there are too many suspects from their various circles that we don't know.'

Sighing, I got up. 'I need food. Jeanette's?'

Beau jumped from the couch. 'Always.'

18

I hear you're sleuthing again

I wasn't actually hungry, but I could use the walk into the village to let all those new insights percolate. In particular, the one that had Thibault ask for my help after he'd already tried to make sense of the situation. As much as I'd wanted to stay away from the murders for Jacqueline's sake, I now wanted to get to the bottom of this for Beau.

But where to start? Not knowing for certain if there was a connection between any of the murders, we should probably look at each of them individually. But that in turn left us with a whole host of suspects, most of whom were as yet unknown to us. For Wylène alone, there could be family and friends, business contacts, past acquaintances... Roméo Paris didn't seem to have been in contact with many outside the commune, but what about his life before he moved there? And don't even get me started on Xavier's clients. We'd first have to find out which of his dealings were legal, and even then, that didn't exclude disgruntled customers.

The hum of people gathered for a drink on the village square drove those thoughts to the back of my mind. I spotted several familiar faces, but faltered in my step when I heard a voice I would recognise anywhere. Mainly because it rose above everything else. The booming laugh of Benoît Le Roux.

My eyes searched for his beard among the crowd, but I found my mother's gauzy, crocheted hairpiece first. I nudged Beau. 'They haven't seen us yet. Do you think we could still—'

'Julieee!'

Oh no. That was even worse. Bella Dudevant had caught me in her talons.

'Amazing party the other day. Absolutely Insta-worthy. We were talking about that to Anne-Bonny, weren't we?' She addressed Isabelle Cochon, the butcher's wife. Those two always appeared together these days. 'By the way, thanks for introducing us. She has *the* best ideas for content. A bit rough, you know, she's so young! Needs a mentor. But I think she'll do well with my guidance. I mean, that scene in the water!'

Oh, you mean that pose she stole from me and performed on my land without me knowing it? Somehow, I doubted Bella's mentoring would put a stop to illegal entry, but before I could think of a fitting retort, Anne-Bonny herself joined us. Her outfit today was understated compared to her usual. A light grey jumpsuit in stretch velour with tight ribbing at the elbows and knees, paired with light-up, see-through plastic platform heels.

'Oh, Isabelle,' she cooed. 'That outfit is gorgeous. Makes you look ten years younger.'

'Don't compliment me on looking young,' Isabelle snapped, and my eyes widened at the unexpected antagonism. 'Everyone knows you're lying, and you're just putting a spotlight on my age. Compliment my outfit, or my hair, or say that I look happy, radiant, ready to go, or even fresh, but Don't. Mention. The years!'

She stormed off, leaving the rest of us blinking. I, for one, was stunned that what she said actually made sense. But Bella got over the shock much more quickly, if she'd been shocked at all. She fluttered her lashes and put on her pout.

'Sooo, Julieee... How *are* you?'

Ah, I was her charity case for the week. That's what you get for breaking down at your own party.

'We've been on the trail of an art forger,' Beau cut in.

Gasping through a wide smile, Bella put her hand on her cleavage, and Anne-Bonny jumped up and down with excitement, setting off a light show in her shoes.

'How exhilarating,' Bella proclaimed. 'You know, I once met an artist. He wanted to experience the agony and the ecstasy of art. Insisted I help him with the ecstasy. I, however, was more inclined to give him agony. I wonder if he ever achieved ecstasy again.'

Both women burst out laughing. Bella gave us a finger wave as she turned towards the café, and Anne-Bonny gave me a quick hug for the sole purpose of giving Beau a long one, leg lifting and all. She didn't even look back at me when she left, so I could indulge in a good head shaking. I heard Beau chuckle, but had to set off towards the café. My mother had spotted us and waved us over.

'He was at my party too,' I quickly informed Beau as we approached *Maman* and Benoît.

He nodded. 'Yeah, I know.'

It made me frown, but I'd already started the next sentence. 'I think he's seeing *Maman*.'

His full-on snort made me stop short.

'What?' He laughed. 'I thought you were such a brilliant detective. He's been seeing her for months. Monsieur Le Roux.' He greeted the man as an old friend.

'Benoît, I keep telling you! *Bonsoir, ma chère.* It's good to see you too.' Benoît held his hand out to me, and I took it slightly dumbfounded. Of course I'd realised there was something going on between the two of them, but how was Thibault so in the know?

I took the chair on the other side of my mother, and Beau pulled one up from the next table over.

My mother put a hand on my arm. 'So, I hear you're sleuthing again—'

'Let's get you a drink,' Benoît interjected. Was he purposely cutting my mother off? If she noticed, she was too busy glaring at me to do anything about it. What had *I* done?

Beau saved me again. 'We're catching a forger.'

'A what? What does that have to do with Chloé?'

'Chloé? What do you mean?' I asked, ignoring Benoît's eye roll.

'I received a lengthy message just now asking me if I could get you to back off! Now, what have you been doing to upset her? She asked for your help, and instead you blame her? Hasn't she been through enough? If you persist in this preposterous pursuit—'

'That's a lot of *p*'s.' I shouldn't have said that. It only made her angrier. She took in more wind to blow at me, but I was quicker. 'All I did was ask her if we could talk, preferably in the Centre de Prédiction. How is that a pursuit?'

Maman deflated. 'Really?'

'Yes, really. And thanks for not checking with me before getting angry.'

'Rosé?' Benoît tried when Jeanette came over.

Both my mother and I nodded, though I was more in the mood for a red. An early summer ponytail headache was brewing, so I pulled out my hair band and freed my thick locks.

'*Alors...* She was quite convincing,' my mother said with a slight blush.

'And you were ready to be convinced.'

'*Tiens*, see for yourself.' She shoved her phone under my nose. 'Lengthy message' was an understatement. Chloé went on and on about how she felt accused by our community (I supposed that's what got to my mother's mayorly pride), and that she would leave and take her business with her, closure or no closure.

'Chloé, hi.' I'd called her before I'd even read the whole thing. 'There seems to have been a misunderstanding.' She went off on a rant that I could let run as Jeanette brought me a glass of red. Bless her instinct! Half the glass was gone before Chloé allowed me to speak. 'So who was this person accusing you? Because I only wanted to talk.' After a few more uh-huhs, I could end with, 'All right, see you tomorrow.'

My mother raised her eyebrows, but I was still miffed enough to let her wait. Jeanette had also brought me a *tarte au légumes* which awakened my hunger. I cut through the flaky sides and relished the tasty mix of olives, tomatoes, courgette, and bell pepper. Three more bites and my mum was on the edge of her seat.

'Someone else had accused her.' She would have to be patient while I devoured more of the savoury *tarte*.

'Who?' Beau asked between forkfuls of a *quiche à l'agneau*. The lamb quiche was one of Beau's favourites.

I put down my fork to get him to look me in the eye. 'Anaëlle.' He frowned, and I continued, 'Apparently, her mother had called her from the Centre de Prédiction to tell her that the same man who had climbed into a window that morning was now talking to Chloé. Since that man was – get this – Alain, Anaëlle thought she had enough to start making accusations.'

That made his jaw drop. Only, he'd still been chewing and had the good manners to keep his mouth shut. The elongated face and tucked-in chin were not the best look on him. He quickly swallowed. 'Alain and Chloé know each other?'

I made an exaggerated shrug with my hands held up to the side. 'I guess? According to Chloé, it was all perfectly innocent, and he'd only come by for some business or other, but Anaëlle had jumped to all kinds of conclusions, saying they were in cahoots against Jessica and that, somehow, this was proof of Chloé being involved in Xavier's murder.' I dropped my hands, reaching for my wine instead. 'But she's agreed to see me tomorrow morning, so hopefully we'll get some answers to the whole bewildering affair.'

'Speaking of...' Beau pointed his fork over my mother's shoulder, who immediately and conspicuously turned in her seat.

Jessica stood by the church door, her flowing skirt flapping in the draft that always blew around the church tower. She was talking to the church cleaner. No Alain in sight.

'So...' *Maman* started, turning back and frowning at her wine, as if it could give her clarity. 'You don't think Chloé did it. And neither did Jessica. Who is this Alain? And Anaëlle? Did they do it?'

I glanced at Thibault before answering. 'We're looking into Richard Othman.'

'What? But he's—'

'Not your jurisdiction,' I reminded her before she could tell me about all his supposed economic benefits to the community. 'He seems to be the only one connected to all three victims in one way or another.'

My mother wrinkled her nose. 'How likely is it to have been some random person we don't know?'

I thought that likelihood was growing by the minute, but Beau grinned. 'As convenient as that might be for your purposes, it's highly unlikely. Three murders so close together, and on one day? And they all have something to do with art.'

'Even Wylène?'

'She, or she and Chloé, had bought a painting from Xavier Grosse the day before.'

Maman pressed her lips together. 'It's thin, but it's there.'

Benoît, who'd kept himself unusually quiet, now joined in with a story about a painting he'd once bought from Xavier. Beau stoked the fire by asking about the art and soon, the three of them were engaged in a lively discussion about why someone would kill an art dealer. My eyes trained on the dancing fabric of Jessica's skirt, I listened without joining in. The connection *was* thin. Could we really be so sure it was there at all? Didn't the pieces fit together better if there were in fact two, or even three separate puzzles to solve?

The connection between artist and dealer was obvious, made even more so by the dealer's rings turning up in the artist's studio, but what if Wylène's death had nothing to do with those two? It could even have been an accident after all. I decided to make it my priority to prove at least that possibility when we visited the Centre de Prédiction in the morning.

19

They still think I did it

Waving at Jessica, I removed myself from the arty conversation. The wave was more for the benefit of my companions because Jessica didn't see me. When I came closer, I heard she was trying to convince the church cleaner to let her in, but the woman had done this job all her life and had appointed herself guardian of the building, going against the inherent openness of the church in trying to keep people out.

'*Coucou*, Madeline,' I greeted the older woman. 'You're working late today.'

'*Bonsoir, Madame.*' I could never get her to use my name, even though I was so much younger. 'There was plenty left to do after those so-called cleaners were done. What do they know about cleaning a church? All they know is crime scenes. Puh!'

'I'm sure you've done a marvellous job at cleaning up their mess. Will you show me?' I winked at Jessica when the woman inflated and turned to unlock the little door nestled into the big wooden church door.

'You're good,' Jessica whispered in my ear as we followed Madeline.

'She's old-fashioned,' I whispered back. 'My family built the church, so in her eyes, it's my church. She would have let me in anyway, but this way is just a bit nicer.'

Our village church, though far too big, was nothing special. Inside, all the requirements for a house of prayer were met, but we didn't have a special Madonna, or a lavishly decorated altar. Even the image of our patron saint was simple. The building itself was reconstructed in 1865, after the original twelfth-century one had been destroyed by some particularly excited revolutionaries in 1793. My ancestor had apparently thought it wise to keep things sober after that particular event.

While Jessica veered off to the right aisle, I followed Madeline down the nave, where she stopped at the centre and pointed to her left.

'That's where he was when I found him. I knew not to start cleaning right away, but I had no idea I'd have to clean up after the cleaners.'

My stomach turned at the thought of standing exactly where the murderer would have been, though the church now looked exactly as it always did. 'You found him? That's horrible. I'm so sorry, Madeline.' I reached out to touch her arm, but she shrugged.

'Violence is a part of life. Just look at the birds of prey in the vineyards. They make a giant mess sometimes. At least this guy didn't spread fur or feathers. Not even paint this time.'

I was about to make a remark on the birds at least killing to eat, but Madeline seemed to have made up her mind about violence. Instead, I asked, 'He came here often?'

'About once a month. Sometimes he copied one of the fourteen *Stations du Chemin de Croix*, but mostly he came to paint the big one.' She pointed her thumb over her shoulder at Saint-Maurice's dubious claim to fame. The huge, once colourful Madonna-queen was supposedly painted by some famous Renaissance artist. My brother had ideas of having it cleaned so we could promote it as an attraction, but the Madelines of Saint-Maurice weren't too happy with that plan. Madeline herself didn't care about the art but didn't want people trampling her clean floors if they didn't come to worship. But a substantial portion of Saint-Maurice's inhabitants simply wanted to keep the work to themselves and didn't care for hordes of tourists flooding the village. These were the people also opposed to Jeanette and me reopening the hotel, so I had first-hand experience dealing with their closed minds. I wished my brother luck.

Jessica joined us, looking up at the dull, brownish picture. 'This is it, *hein*?' She contemplated the art before her, clearly looking for what made it so special. 'I don't see it. But then, I do sculpture, not paintings.'

I cast one last look around, but the church looked the same as it had done since I was a child. If the killer had left behind any evidence, it had been thoroughly removed already. Apart maybe from the psychological evidence that this killer clearly thought nothing of the sanctuary the church was supposed to provide.

The three of us filed out of the little door, which Madeline locked behind us. I thanked her and she scurried off around the tower.

'What do you think?' I asked Jessica, gesturing with my head to the church behind us.

She shrugged. 'Oh, it's not really my style. I'd heard about that painting from people in the commune, but usually when I come here, the church is closed. It was actually closed now, too, of course, so thanks for helping me in.'

I inclined my head by way of answer. 'How are things?' I asked as we moved out of the draft towards Jeanette's café.

She huffed a humourless laugh. 'They still think I did it.'

'Don't worry. Capitaine Gavel knows you're my friend. You may be their best lead right now, but she won't let her colleague arrest you unless they have really solid evidence.'

'They won't find any against *me*, but now I'm not so sure about Alain.'

'I heard about that. Sort of. What did happen?'

She raised her eyebrows at me, then shook her curls. 'News travels fast. Long story short: he wasn't who I thought he was, so I kicked him out.'

Benoît and my mother had left, so we joined Beau at his table.

'You kicked out the millionaire?' he asked.

'The what?' Jessica laughed heartily. 'That's a good one.'

Beau and I exchanged a look while we ordered another round of drinks. 'Good riddance, anyway,' I said, nodding to underline my point. 'I didn't trust him one bit.'

Jessica stared at the stem of the glass she was playing with. 'I know. It all seemed so random that I thought he couldn't possibly be involved. He couldn't have known I'd be there to pick him up, right? Or that I would let him stay. But then why would he have me pick up an envelope from the exact same place whose owner I'm suspected to have murdered? While he goes off to sneak in a window somewhere! That doesn't look honest at all. Especially now that I've inherited the building he wants to rent.'

'You did? Why would Xavier have left you a whole building? He must have liked you more than you thought.' This was an interesting new development. But it didn't look good for Jessica, since it gave her motive.

She shrugged. 'Looks more like an admittance of guilt to me. For a moment, I actually thought he knew he was going to get murdered and did it to spite me. But that was too outrageous, even for me. I just wish there was a way of proving my innocence. But I have no alibi, a whole bunch of possible murder weapons – which, by the way, I'm never ever making another one of – and my motive is growing stronger by the day.'

She slumped forward, resting her forehead on crossed arms on the table. 'I know I shouldn't pick up strange men and let them stay in my house. I knew that before I did it. I keep hoping there will be an innocent explanation for what he did. I know he lied to me... But I still miss him.'

She straightened and dug into a pocket in her skirt, pulling out a little rubber balloon-like ball with a tube on one end. 'He left this. Don't know if it's important, but I've no idea how to get it back to him. I don't even know what it is.'

'It's a puffer,' I said in my best Brainy Smurf voice. 'You use it to blow dust from hard-to-reach places, like inside a camera.'

'Or to blow dust on places you've tampered with, like planting a bug for spying on someone.'

I narrowed my eyes at Beau, remembering Maile's story but also still not believing it. 'Really.'

Jessica uttered the same word, but with a different intonation. Her eyes widened at the little tool. 'Really? I guess that would fit with him sneaking into a window. And with the paint on his finger.'

I rolled my eyes.

'You don't honestly believe a guy worth that much would be involved with clandestine operations? And you just happened to pick him up on the day that you're accused of a murder he just happens to be involved with? Somehow? I mean, that's a stretch, even for you.' I flicked my hand at Beau, who shrugged.

'What do you mean, worth that much?'

'Oh, Jess...' I sighed, pulling up Alain's name on my phone and showing her the search results. 'Trusting people is great, but having a base for that trust is probably better.'

Her jaw dropped as she scrolled. 'I kicked out a millionaire? But what was he doing walking down that road? Pretending to be a builder? And why did he climb in a window at the Centre de Prédiction?'

'Now those are valid questions,' I answered as I got my phone back and stared at the handsome face of Alain Coquard adorning an article on people with good business sense. 'Did he say or do anything that could link him to Xavier? Or to Chloé, for that matter?'

Jessica winced. 'Yes? Although I'm not sure how it's all connected, really.'

Grinning, Beau leaned forward. 'Spill.'

'Well...' She rubbed her hands on her skirt. 'I said I was going into Villefranche for groceries and so he asked me to pick up some paperwork at Xavier's. He said he'd done some building work for him but that he was in between projects at the moment. It sounded okay to me. How was I supposed to know?'

'Did you look at the papers?' I asked, ignoring her attempt at justification. Her naïveté made me feel like the most jaded person in the world. I sure had my reasons not to trust people, which sometimes made me long for a bit more innocence, but now I wondered how someone like Jessica had made it this far without growing suspicious of people. But then, her art had been stolen by her ex-boyfriend, for whose murder she was now a prime suspect, and still she trusted a random man off the street to tell her the truth. Some people just had it in them.

'No.' She kept her eyes on her lap as she fiddled with her nails. 'They weren't mine. I didn't want to snoop, so I gave him the envelope without checking its contents.'

'Did you use his name to get them?' Beau asked.

Jessica shook her head. 'No, he used the name of his company. What was it? Something like Falafel... No, Shish-Kebab! Weird name for a construction company, but that was it.'

'I thought he was a fashion guy. Why would he also be in construction?' I mused.

Jessica huffed. 'Maybe he was like Xavier, making money wherever he could. I do seem to pick 'em.'

'So did he explain why he was going into Chloé Walkure's window?' Beau asked.

Planting her elbows on the table, Jessica put her head in her hands and sighed. 'He said she was a business connection and they wouldn't let him in the front door. But Anaëlle said that was rubbish because she could get in without a glitch, so... I didn't know what to think, and Anaëlle can be quite persuasive, *tu sais*?'

I glanced at Beau. 'Chloé's business is property. It might make sense if Alain does have a construction company?'

'Already on it.' He looked up from his phone. 'Nothing so far, though. No mention of a construction company called Shish-Kebab with the Chamber of Commerce either.'

'I would love to talk with Alain about all this. Do you have his number?'

From inside her hands, Jessica groaned. 'No. Deleted it.'

'Okay.' I pursed my lips. 'We're going to speak to Chloé tomorrow. Perhaps she'll have some answers instead. Maybe we can also have another look at the art while we're there,' I added to Beau. 'See if the paintings they have could be fakes. They have one of yours too,' I said, turning back to Jessica.

She looked up. 'What, a fake?'

'Oh.' I blinked. 'I don't know. I saw one of your spiky things and assumed...'

'I never sold one to the Centre de Prédiction. They could have acquired it from someone else, I suppose, but Othman was a good friend of Xavier's. On the other hand, that probably means Xavier wouldn't stick him with a fake. Do you think you could find out the serial number? I always put numbers on the bottom. I like to keep track of where my babies go.'

Trying to hide my surprise at such organisation from my flighty friend, I nodded. 'We'll see what we can do.'

Beau had another question. 'Other than Alain, though, can you think of anyone who might have killed Xavier?'

Biting her lip, Jessica thought about that. 'If it were just him, the list would have been endless. After he died, Yvonne found out I wasn't the first person he'd scammed, even in his art business alone. But if you add in Roméo Paris and maybe that other girl, I just can't think of anyone. You'd have to look at the list of people who bought one of Roméo's paintings, I guess, but how that links to some girl in the Centre...'

'Wylène Chiche,' Beau muttered.

'Right. She's the odd one out, isn't she?'

We fell silent after that, sipping our drinks. Again, I wondered if Jessica was right. Were all three murders connected just because of their proximity in space and time? I hoped Chloé could clear up some of the questions we had when we'd visit the following day.

Staring over my glass, my eyes following Anne-Bonny as she crossed the square to meet someone, I stiffened. I must have gasped, too, because Beau sat up straight.

'What?'

'Cyprien,' I whispered, my heart racing.

'Where?'

I nodded towards the couple, who were having a friendly chat.

'Who are they?' Jessica asked.

'My neighbour and someone from my past I'd rather never see again,' I answered. 'He put his name down with the local real estate agent six months ago, but I heard nothing of him actually moving here.'

'Seems to know your neighbour, though.' She took another sip. 'You think that's why he's here?'

I downed my drink. 'I think I'm going to go.'

Beau jumped up to pay Jeanette while I pushed my chair out. I glanced towards Anne-Bonny, who made a gesture that triggered a memory of one of her social media posts. 'She knew where I lived before she moved here.'

Jessica frowned, and I explained. 'She copied one of my poses, but she took the picture in the little stream at the bottom of my garden. I thought it was a bit odd when I found out, but I was also flattered, to be honest. But... what if it had nothing to do with her being a fan of my work? What if she's there to spy on me for Franck?' My voice broke when I spoke his name.

Beau, who'd heard the last sentence on his return, took me by the shoulders. 'We're leaving. Talk to you later, Jess.'

'Okay... Bye?' Looking confused and worried, she uttered one last question. 'Who's Franck?'

20

Busy chap

Beau had retreated to his studio after making sure I wasn't too spooked. I'd gone to bed early after talking to Léon, thinking I'd sleep off the shakes, but sleep wouldn't come. Could it be true that Anne-Bonny was part of Franck's network? I'd suspected people before, but Beau had laughed away those fears. He hadn't done that this time. Léon had also tried to put into perspective the significance of Anne-Bonny knowing Cyprien, but he hadn't succeeded in convincing me.

Still, this was Anne-Bonny! The girl who wore extravagant clothes and thought the 1920s were 'the actual days of the pirates'. Was all that just a very convincing act? And even though she was my neighbour, what could she possibly tell Franck about me? Our houses weren't within view of each other and we weren't on drop-in terms. The only time I'd invited her was to show her the studio, since we were both effectively in portrait photography. She'd gushed over my set-up, and we'd exchanged some tips – craft and business from me and marketing from her – but we weren't close in any sense of the word.

But then why had she seemed so friendly with my ex-husband's closest crony? As far as I knew, he didn't live in the village. If not for me, why was he here? I remembered my mother's words when I'd first seen his name on some papers with the local estate agent. She'd suggested he'd found a girl he liked and he might want to settle down away from Villefranche and 'the business'. But that couldn't be Anne-Bonny, because she'd moved here afterwards and I hadn't seen Cyprien since.

Sighing, I threw off the covers. Sleep was too much to ask for. These same thoughts had been going round and round in my mind for at least an hour now, and though I was tired *of* them, I wasn't tired enough to fall asleep. Not even putting my fingers to my forehead and pulling the worries out would work this time of night. Perhaps if I focussed on other people's problems, I would forget about my own.

Traipsing down the stairs, I plucked a fuzzy blanket from the basket by the couch and switched on my tablet while I made a nest for myself. Seeing Cyprien had driven all thoughts of the murders from my mind, but now I concentrated on Jessica's remark. 'She's the odd one out', she'd said about Wylène. I'd considered the possibility that two of the murders could be connected while one was not, but hadn't examined it seriously. First, though, I'd have another look to see if I would end up with different suspects if I treated all the murders as separate occasions.

First up, Wylène Chiche. She was the odd one out, and the most important to me because she was the most important to Beau. He'd asked me specifically to look into her murder, so that's where I'd start. The problem was that I didn't know anything about her. A quick search only told me what I already knew: she was Chloé Walkure's assistant. Every single picture of her showed the two of them together. It was almost as if she didn't have a life of her own. Wasn't that what Beau had said too? She'd talked about her work a little and about Chloé a little more, but she hadn't mentioned anything personal.

I scanned through a few articles praising the rapid rise of Chloé's business and the unconventional choices she'd made to get her to this point, but none of them mentioned Wylène other than in her role of inseparable assistant. Even the older articles from when Chloé had been relatively obscure didn't give any personal background. One article mentioned neither woman had any living relatives and that's what brought them so close together, but since the author had mixed up their ages, calling Wylène the older one, I doubted I could take the information at face value. Another thing I'd have to ask Chloé.

Since the internet couldn't help me with Wylène, I moved on to Xavier. I was sure there'd be loads of information on him online and I was right. There was so much that I had to unpick the threads to find an end to pull to unravel the whole mess. The end I found was Jessica. She'd downplayed her role in Xavier's career, or at least in the art part of it. According to what I found, he'd already been a valid player in several other fields, but his art gallery had been a sideline to his business until he started flogging Jessica's art.

Overnight, the art went from sideline to the main focus of Xavier's entrepreneurial spirit. Almost all pictures of his handsome, jovial face were relatively recent, taken at events that opened new doors for him and brought him into contact with high rollers in areas of business where he did not yet have a foot on the ground.

One article, published only the day before, was especially interesting. A local reporter by the name of Pascal Gateau had written an exposé showcasing all the different ways in which Xavier had bent and brazenly broken the law. Jessica had already told me about the fakes, of course, and Anaëlle had hinted at overvaluing and money laundering, but this reporter had done some digging into Xavier's dealings outside of the gallery and had uncovered tax evasion, shell companies, and investment scams as well.

I looked up from my screen. 'Busy chap.' How much of all that criminal behaviour would Richard Othman, who claimed to have been his best friend, have known about? Were they in it together, or had Richard found out and disagreed so strongly that he'd killed Xavier? And if not Richard, who else could be a suspect? Looking at the list of crimes Pascal Gateau had revealed, the number of people involved could indeed be endless, as Jessica had warned me. Perhaps the timing of the murder could still be significant, even if it wasn't connected to the other two. But how?

Pulling my blanket tighter around my shoulders, I gave up on Xavier for now. Too little information for Wylène, too much for Xavier. Maybe Roméo Paris would be Goldilocks, but given how much I'd found when I searched his name earlier, I doubted it. Nevertheless, I typed in his name, and a few new hits appeared. All they had to say, however, was that Roméo had died, leaving behind his daughter and a barnful of paintings.

I yawned. Two hours had passed and I hadn't found anything useful. At least I was a bit tired by now. Even thinking about Cyprien didn't bother me as much as it had earlier. All right, one last search. A long shot. I typed in 'Piguemal'. It still struck me as odd that an artist as broadly accomplished as Roméo Paris had chosen to only fake Piguemal paintings when it would have been much less conspicuous to copy a wide variety of artists.

I had to scroll through several pages of paintings before I found a portrait of the artist. Not a painted self-portrait, but a vague, grainy photograph. The photo manipulation apps I had on my tablet weren't nearly as powerful as those on my work computer, but I managed to improve the picture somewhat nonetheless.

A gaunt man in his thirties stared at me. He had a scraggly beard and longish, reddish hair, and looked as if he wanted to be anywhere but captured in that moment. Squinting at the photo, I tried to imagine him without the beard, or maybe just a moustache. Shorter hair? Older? As I went through the changes in my mind, my eyes widened and I reached for my phone.

Jacqueline picked up on the third ring. *'De quoi?!'*

'Roméo Paris is Régis Piguemal. Or he was. That's why he faked only Piguemal paintings. He *was* him.'

A faint snoring sound came over the line.

'Jacqueline!'

'De quoi?!'

'Did you hear what I said?'

'Ouai... yeah. In the morning, okay?' She hung up before I could answer, but at least I'd done my bit. I helped. I wasn't sure how this would be useful in finding his killer, but I was sure it was significant.

Feeling perhaps a little too proud of my relatively small discovery, I dragged myself back upstairs and was asleep in minutes.

21

This place is no fun any more

'Thibault, I'm leaving! The hair looks fine.' I added the last bit in a mumble, since from the bottom of the stairs, I couldn't see what he was doing, but I had my suspicions. Jacqueline had sent me a text that she would follow up on my discovery, so I was doubly determined to help her out where she couldn't investigate.

Beau came sailing down the stairs. 'All right, let's go.'

He was in my car telling me to hurry before I'd even shut the door. I yawned, not at all feeling compelled to hurry on his account. On the way to the Centre de Prédiction, I told him about my discovery the night before. His eyes started to sparkle.

'You mean my Piguemal is real after all? That's it, I'm picking it up from the gallery on our way back.'

Feeling oh so satisfied with myself at having been able to hand him this precious gift twice now, I still had the feeling there was something else I should tell him about. Tapping the wheel while trying to remember, I stopped to let a mother and child cross the road. I smiled, suppressing another yawn. Whatever it was that had seemed so important a moment ago was skipping away with the child on her mother's hand. The cheery spring sun wasn't helping me feel any more awake after my midnight research, either. Perhaps I should join those people playing *pétanque*.

What was it I needed to say? A handsome man all dressed in black, a backpack slung over his shoulder, leaned against the old wooden wine press that decorated the entrance to the village on the Blacenas road, finding shelter under its roof against the sun that was making me squint. Not able to put my finger on the no longer important memory, I instead listed all the things we were supposed to ask and look out for at the Centre. 'Jacquie's boss has closed Wylène's case as an accident, despite Chloé's objections. But you said it wasn't, and Jacqueline couldn't find the *grattons* or the pills, so we'll have to see if we can get into her room. See if there is any place the police might have overlooked. And then we should probably ask about Wylène's family and friends, and specifically if she had any enemies.'

'But if she did, Chloé would have said so by now, right?'

'Mm, yes, so maybe we have to push a little. Clients or business partners that might have acted friendly because they wanted something but could have some kind of grievance, that sort of thing. But we also have to find out about Alain and why he was sneaking in through a window.'

'And check the serial number on Jessica's artwork.'

'Right.' I turned into the Centre's car park and tried to rub my eyes without dislodging my false lashes. 'Now hope they let us in.'

'No problem.' Beau was already on his way to the entrance, and I had to hurry to catch up. 'We have an appointment with Chloé Walkure,' he declared to the intercom. 'Richard said to keep it quiet, so I suggest you let us in quickly.'

Mimicking Beau's disinterested arrogance, I watched the desk clerk reach for the phone, then think better of it and open the doors.

'Monsieur Othman knows you're here?'

'Of course,' Beau said.

'We know where to go.' I strode past the desk with a haughtiness that made Beau pinch my arm when we'd rounded the corner.

'Look at you! I'm proud of you, young Padawan. Though, of course, you have much to learn.' He laughed. 'So... you know where to go?'

'Just making a little detour.' Disguising the fact that I only knew how to find the art gallery via Moira's room, I knocked on her door as if that had always been my intention.

When Moira opened the door, she was dressed to go out, jacket already zipped up. Her suitcase was sitting on the bed behind her.

'Oh! Sorry, I didn't expect you,' she said. 'Come on in.'

'We're not really here to see you,' I explained as she closed the door behind us. 'Just wanted to ask you a few things. But you're leaving?'

Moira shrugged. 'This place is no fun any more. All the crazy glamour is gone. Half the people have already left and the others are just going through the motions because they've spent a fortune and are determined to get their money's worth. That's not me. I'm going to stay with Marie for a few days, until my plane leaves. What is it you wanted to ask?'

'I see. First, how hard was it to smuggle in those crisps you were talking about?'

She raised her eyebrows. 'My crisps? Not hard at all. It's not like they search your luggage when you arrive. They give you a massive list of rules on what you should and shouldn't bring, but nobody checks it. That all?'

'You know that painting you bought for your dad? Could I have a look at it?'

Her face fell. 'Oh. No, I'm sorry. I already sent it by post. Was there something wrong with it, or...?'

Realising it was a bit of an odd request, I shook my head. 'Nothing to do with you or the painting, but do you remember the name of the artist?'

'Sure. It was Paris. I had to explain to Dad that I hadn't gone to Paris but that it was the name of the artist. And here I was thinking he knew about art.'

I smiled. 'Do you remember if you showed your painting to Wylène Chiche?'

'Who? The dead girl?'

Beau shifted his weight to the other foot. Moira couldn't know he'd felt close to Wylène, of course, but hearing Moira talk about her so casually made even me uncomfortable. I hastened to repeat, 'Yes. Did you show her?'

Moira wiggled her mouth while she thought. 'I think so... Yes, actually, I'm sure. She admired it and said it was very similar to the one she'd bought. That was all, though. Not much of a conversation.'

'Thanks.' I smiled. 'Hope the rest of your holiday will be more fun.'

She huffed. 'I'm sure it will. I've eaten enough yoghurt to last me a lifetime.'

She left the room with us but went the other way with a wave of her hand.

'Do you think Wylène could have spotted the similarities between the Paris and the Piguemal?' I asked Beau as we wandered the corridors.

'I don't know. Maybe. Is that important?'

I pursed my lips, still feeling my way around my thoughts through the fog in my head while trying to remember if I turned right or left at this wobbly egg statue. 'I'm still not sure whether all these cases are linked or not. I wanted to know if there was a connection, just in case.' Another wobbly egg, this one leaning to the left instead. Had I seen that one already? The corridors were even more deserted than last time, so there was no one to ask. And signs were probably considered detrimental to The Experience. One more of these unknown turns, however, and Beau would find out I had no idea where we were.

'Chloé! How are you?' Suddenly wide awake, I drew back after having almost bumped into the very person we were here to see. This was the second time I'd found her in the corridors instead of having to locate her room.

'Fine, thanks.' She gave the polite answer to the polite question, but it was obvious she was not all right. She wore the Centre's robe, but it had a coffee stain on the lapel which she tried to hide under the shoulder strap of her purse. Her slippers were mismatched and an ugly rash showed at her hairline. As she led us down the corridor to her room, she babbled, 'It's just... I didn't realise how much I'd come to rely on Wylène. Without her... I may have to sell the business. That wasn't part of the plan, but... All these people want things that I don't know about. I thought I knew. I didn't think she kept things from me. We were so close.'

I stepped closer and rubbed her arm, though I really wanted to hug her. The confident woman I'd met a few days ago had annoyed me at first, but this incoherent human being she'd been replaced with could only be pitied. The message my mother had received made more sense now too. If Anaëlle had let loose on Chloé when she was in this state, anything could have come out.

As she led us to her room, Chloé scratched her head, and I asked, 'Are you allergic to one of the products?'

She looked me in the eye, and suddenly the old Chloé returned. She straightened and lifted her chin. 'It must be stress. I made a deal with Richard that I'd come here and provide him with some publicity, but only if I were allowed to bring my laptop and phone. That's normally against the rules, and I can now see why. I think I will hand them over after all and take the time I need to grieve and to recover. Thank you for letting me see that.'

She took a small step away from me as she opened her door, creating enough space that it would be awkward for me to rub her arm again. The room looked similar to Moira's, sparsely decorated in white with some wood accents, but the bed had not been made and was strewn with papers, a few pens, a half open laptop, and two phones.

'We actually came to talk to you about Wylène. This is Thibault, who was with her before she died. I believe you've met?'

'Briefly, yes.' She smiled at Beau, who nodded.

I looked around for somewhere to sit, but there was only one chair, and Chloé didn't make any attempts at making either us or herself more comfortable. 'We were wondering if you could tell us a bit more about Wylène's relatives and friends, as well as her professional relationships. I take it you still believe her death was not an accident?'

Chloé cast down her gaze and pressed her lips together. 'I'm not sure what to believe any more. Surely the police know more about these things than I do? And I just can't think of anyone who would have wanted to hurt poor Wylène. It makes no sense. So... maybe I have to accept that this was her own decision, and let it go.'

I glanced at Beau. If Chloé herself wanted to leave this awful event behind her, who were we to pursue our investigation?

'Would you mind if we had a look at her room nonetheless?' he asked.

Chloé shrugged. 'Why not. We had adjoining rooms, so I can let you in through here.'

Beau and I spent less than five minutes examining the room. The bed had been made and anything lying around had been removed either by the police or afterwards. The one cupboard held only clothes and the bedside table was empty. Beau even checked the walls and ceiling, but couldn't find any hidden compartments or loose panels.

'Someone must have come in and taken the container for the *grattons* away after she ate them. Most likely the killer.' I turned to Chloé, who took a step back.

'Don't look at me. I was hiking with you.'

'I know. I was going to ask, do you know who found her?'

'Oh, one of the nurses, I think. Someone heard strange noises coming from the room, so they alerted the staff. I don't remember who it was.'

I sighed. Neither Chloé nor the room could provide us with any more clues on the death of Wylène Chiche. Perhaps I had to let go of this one too. I winced when I looked at Beau, whose defeated slouch conveyed a similar realisation.

'I guess there's nothing more for us to do,' I said to Chloé, who tried to suppress a shiver.

'Thank you for trying. And thank you,' she added to Beau, 'for making her last hours so enjoyable.'

Beau gave a curt nod. We should leave. If I'd had any moral grounds to ask around before, I certainly didn't now. And yet...

'How do you know Alain Coquard?'

Chloé rolled her eyes. 'Not this again. I met him at a fundraiser ages ago. Suddenly, he shows up here yesterday, far too eager to get into business with me. I spoke to him for five minutes and then I sent him away, but that ridiculous woman had to make it into something sordid. Everyone knows she's not all there, and that daughter of hers is well on her way too.'

Not wanting to upset her more, we started to say our goodbyes, but Chloé interrupted.

'Could I ask you a favour, Beau? There's a surprise sale on at the artists' commune. One of the other guests was talking about it earlier. Wylène had wanted to go to the commune to check out the local artists, so I want to go in her honour and buy as many suitable pieces as I can find. I could use a pair of strong arms there, and I gather you have an eye for art yourself?'

'*Bof,*' was his unusually non-committal answer. 'If Julie doesn't need me.'

'Go ahead.'

'Wonderful! Give me twenty minutes to freshen up, and I'll meet you at the entrance.'

He nodded and left the room, but Chloé held me back when I wanted to follow.

'Say, you and Beau...?'

I suppressed an eye roll. 'No.' How many times would I have to tell people? 'Goodbye, Chloé.'

Thibault frowned when I joined him on the way to the art room. 'What did she want that's got your petticoats in a twist?'

'To know if I had any sort of claim on you,' I grumbled.

'Oh.'

I glanced up at him. 'Doesn't that bother you?'

He only shrugged and kept walking.

'She's supposed to be grieving for her best friend, but instead she wants to go after a man half her age.'

'Life goes on.'

'But...' I paused for a few steps to formulate my next question delicately. 'You're not... interested, though. Are you?'

He stopped dead in his tracks and I skidded to a halt. 'Just because I understand doesn't mean I feel the same way. And even if I did, what business is that of yours? You're starting to sound like my mother.'

Wow. As much as I liked his mother, I didn't think he could have insulted me more right then. We walked to the art room in silence, not bothering to be stealthy about it.

'Let's just verify the serial number and get out of here,' I said as we entered the large round space.

'Good idea.' He strode up to Jessica's piece and lifted it for me to take a photo, which I sent off to Jess.

'What are you doing?! That's a very valuable piece of art!' Richard Othman's voice echoed around the room.

'Busted,' Beau said under his breath while he carefully replaced the statue.

'Not according to this.' I held up my phone so Othman could see Jessica's reply: *FAKE!* He winced but didn't seem surprised. 'The artist kept a record of her work but never told the forger – and we both know who we're talking about – what her system was. Apparently, his guess was wrong.'

Othman rubbed his left eye, then dropped his hand to his side. 'All right. You'd better come to my office.'

Beau and I exchanged a look as we followed him. Through Beau's earlier frustration I could now see curiosity starting to surface. Remembering his earlier assertion that Othman must be the killer, I wondered if he could be right. Othman would have had access to Wylène's room. He was a known friend of Xavier's and if Jessica's art here was fake, perhaps the Piguemal was... What to call it – quasi-fake? But even if he did have a connection to all three victims, what could possibly have been his motive?

Othman's office was an extension of the rest of the building. The same organic, egg-white shapes in furnishings, same soft lighting, same taupey colour on the walls. Only his desk was out of place. An oversized, antique statement piece in dark walnut, it dominated the room and made it feel small. Othman took a seat in the egg-white swivel chair behind it and instantly seemed two feet shorter. If he wanted to impress anyone, he'd chosen the wrong furniture. If, however, he wanted to be unimposing to make people feel at ease, perhaps he'd made a very strategic choice. Which was it?

'I will tell you what I know, but I will deny any of it should you feel inclined to make this story public.' He held his hand out to each of us in turn, keeping his other hand on the arm rest. Neither of us agreed, but he'd made his declaration.

'It all started as a joke,' he began, leaning back with his eyes closed. I exchanged a look with Beau. Were we in for a confession? 'Xavier and I, we knew we had a gift for talking people into things. Even at university, he used it to get out of assignments, and I used it to get girls. One day, he bought a disgusting old doll at a *vide-grenier*, a flea market, and bet me that he could sell it at some ridiculous price, like a few hundred euros. I laughed in his face and said I'd believe that when I saw it. But... he made it happen. That was the first time we thought we could make a living with words.

'We were careful not to do anything illegal back then. We just... made things look a little better than they were, but we could always back up our claims. That land we sold could indeed be valuable for construction... if they only put in the money to have the old factory that now occupied it demolished. It was all in the contracts, but we talked them into signing without reading.'

The back of the chair pressed into my shoulder blades. Without realising it, I'd leaned back from Othman. Wherever he was going with this, it reminded me all too keenly of that time in my own life when I'd fallen for words without examining too closely what was behind them. What was it Othman was trying to achieve with this explanation?

'That kind of thing, though, it doesn't make you popular. We needed to find ways to improve the value in the eye of the beholder. Xavier went into art, and I turned to wellness. He could sell the ugliest painting with a good story. I always made sure people felt good about coming to my Centre before they'd even started any of the treatments. We sold them *air au gratin* for literal mountains of gold sometimes.

'But gradually, we began to see the merit of what we sold. Or at least, I did. People genuinely feel better when they leave this place. I began to see them less as suckers and more as people with a void I could fill. A large part of that is still the story I sell them, but I don't consider my words empty any more. They're therapeutic, even if they build up the experience to more than it essentially is. And people pay me for that experience.'

'Hm.' He only had me half-convinced, if that. I knew like no other that the experience can be worth more than the final product, but would Othman be shrewd enough to use that against me? He was an admitted smooth talker, so I had to be careful what I believed. 'And Xavier? Did he see the intrinsic value of the art?'

Othman gave a sly laugh. 'He learned what kind of art was worth more, if that counts. He was never satisfied with spinning tales about art and artists. He wanted to 'test his talent', as he called it. If you ask me, he missed the thrill of talking people into buying something they didn't actually want. Always looking to see if he could get away with another hustle. He sold crazy green energy schemes for a while that turned out to be so black, people were seeing red. Then he tried out the property market, cryptocurrency, and gadgets. And all the while, he honed his craft. So much so, that even I fell for his spiel.'

Ah, he was going for a victim angle. We weren't here for a confession after all, then.

He sighed and stared at a point above the door. 'We had a deal that I would display some of the art from his gallery in my own art room. Like I told you before, art can be therapeutic because it elicits emotions. But sometimes, patrons would become so enamoured with a piece that they'd want to acquire it, which Xavier, of course, was happy enough to facilitate.

'But then his girlfriend at the time became the hottest thing in the art world and she couldn't keep up with demand. You'd think that would keep prices high, but Xavier wanted to cash in on the wave before it passed. He fed her work into a generator and printed out similar pieces. Somehow, he convinced me that it was the style people were after, and that he would give her a bigger cut on the originals, and it would all be okay.'

He threw his hands up in defeat but then straightened. 'Fortunately, I can say I never sold the one piece he lent me. Some of my clients are drawn to it at first, but they don't grow attached to the anger and frustration her pieces represent, since those are exactly the emotions they come here to leave behind.'

'Are any of the other works fake?' I asked.

Othman started to shake his head, but then he froze and looked me in the eye. 'He sold other fakes? I always assumed he'd do me the courtesy of informing me, like he did with the Jessica Rose, but I never questioned the provenance of the other works.' He sighed again, this one a little more genuine and less rehearsed. 'It only goes to show that though I might have had a motive for this abominable crime, executing it would only have highlighted an aspect of my personal history I'm not eager to make public.'

'Unfortunately for you, whoever did execute it has put you in the spotlight after all. The authorities are looking into Monsieur Grosse's dealings. I expect there will be a paper trail leading to you at some point.' Technically, I had only seen a reporter's piece on this, but the police were sure to follow.

Perhaps if I embellished this truth a little, I could get Othman to sweat under his turban.

He inclined his head. 'Thank you for the advance warning, though I can only be blamed for allowing a fake Jessica Rose into the premises. I will contact Madame Rose and personally apologise. Perhaps I can convince her to sell me an original instead.'

'Did you know Wylène Chiche?' Beau asked. We both turned to him at this sudden change of subject.

'Err, no. Well, only as Madame Walkure's assistant. I assume she was the one who booked their stay, but I don't concern myself with such logistics. She seemed more excited about staying here than Madame Walkure was when I gave them their introductory tour, but other than that, I really can't tell you anything about her. I'm afraid her death impacted both me and the Centre more than her life did.'

'How do you mean?' I asked. 'Because of the bad publicity?'

He wiggled his turbaned head. 'For the Centre, yes, that has had an impact. But I am not a heartless businessman, Madame Belmain. The fact that a pretty young woman would feel compelled to take diet pills when she wants to eat fatty foods affects me deeply. I have been going through all our material with a fine-tooth comb to make sure we do not send negative or even ambiguous messages about body image. We are a wellness centre, not a beauty or health clinic. We set rules about what we would like people to eat to make them feel better, not for slimming purposes. That is also why we don't check what people bring in. We're not a prison. We just want to help.'

And make lots of money in the process. Still, I found myself convinced by most of his speech. He had a way with words, but could he really have faked the emotion he'd shown just now?

I couldn't think of anything else to ask, and Beau kept quiet too.

Othman made one last attempt at ensuring our silence. 'You'll understand, any hint of a scandal surrounding the Centre will harm its positive effects on my visitors.'

We said our goodbyes and made our way to the entrance. Beau raked a hand through his hair. 'I hate to say it, but I believe him. There goes my best suspect.'

'Hm.' We still had Anaëlle. 'Don't you think it's odd that they're having a sale so soon after losing one of their community members?'

He gave a small, confused shake of his head before he followed my jump. 'Who? The artists in the commune? Maybe they need to raise money for the funeral?'

'According to Anaëlle, Paris had plenty of money, which should now all be Rosa's.' We turned the last corner. Chloé was waiting at the entrance on the other side of the corridor, closely guarded by yet another bespectacled topknot-wearer behind the front desk. They certainly went for consistency around here. I bumped Beau's arm with mine in that way I'd seen gossipy people do it. 'And I'll tell you something else. That rash is definitely not from stress.'

'How do you know?'

'I used to run a successful beauty blog, remember? People came to me with all kinds of skincare-related issues. That rash is from a hair tonic or a shampoo she hasn't properly rinsed out.'

He sighed, unable to find any enthusiasm for sleuthing after our investigation of Wylène's death had failed. 'How is this relevant? Look, I'm going with her to the commune, anyway. If there's something going on, I'll let you know. I'll see you later, Juju.'

He touched my arm, which I took to mean he was okay. Or he would be. At least he didn't seem inclined to run off again. But... now that I thought about it... Beau had run off before he could possibly have known about Wylène's death. He'd said he couldn't come to my party when he apologised after he was shot, and he'd let me think that Wylène's death was the reason. If it wasn't, did that mean he still might have cause to take off again?

Perhaps it was time for me to let go as well. Of Beau as well as of sleuthing. I'd only ignored Jacqueline's wishes for Beau's sake, and if he was giving up, I had no business poking my nose in these murder cases. Did I?

22

I never thought it would come between us

The man in front of Jessica hardly dared look at her. Whatever she'd expected this morning when she received a text saying *Please let me explain*, this wasn't it.

'But… why?' she finally managed.

Alain shrugged. 'I like a challenge. I told you I like winter and water sports. None of those things I said were untrue. I wouldn't call myself a thrill-seeker, but I like an edge to the things I do. Up to the moment I looked into your building's owner, I was genuinely looking for a place to start a new business, and enjoying your company in the process. But when I saw there was something dodgy about that building, I wanted to find out what was going on. Since they knew me at the gallery, I err… I did lie about that and I'm sorry. I never thought it would come between us before we had a chance to become "us". That's what I'm really sorry about.'

Jessica cast her gaze down and smiled. Not that she was feeling particularly demure, but he wasn't the only one who could pretend. Before they could explore whether there could be an 'us', however, something else needed to be done. 'I think you should tell Julie about all this. Maybe it's connected to Xavier's death. Since I asked for her help, I should give her all the information I have. Or, you have, in this case.'

He nodded, the hopeful smile fading. Well, now that she had his number again, he could wait. Served him right.

'Julie? Are you home? Can we meet you there? It might be important.' Putting the phone down, she bit her bottom lip as she looked at Alain and pondered... No, not yet. Julie was waiting for them. 'I'll drive.'

'Oh, it's you.' Julie looked at Alain as if he'd gone mouldy.

For some reason, this pleased Jessica more than it should. She was back to liking Alain, but it still irked her that he'd lied to her and made her believe he was someone else. 'Don't worry, he's here to explain.'

'Can't wait,' Julie muttered.

She led them to the living room and sat in a comfy chair opposite the sofa that Jessica and Alain took. Her cat jumped on her lap, and she stroked it like a cartoon villain. 'All right, Mister Millionaire, explain.'

Alain laughed, a glorious sound. Jessica sneaked a glance at her couchfellow, who was, again, as confident and laid-back as ever.

'I thought taking in people without looking them up was novel,' he said. 'But I haven't met many people who were that unimpressed with the money. Can I ask you, though, have you found out anything about Xavier Grosse's murder?'

Julie stared at the cat in her lap and sighed. 'A little. Not enough. I keep feeling I'm missing something that's staring me in the face, but I can't put my finger on it. First I thought all three murders were connected, but though Xavier's rings turned up at Roméo's studio, connecting those two, Wylène's death is the odd one out. And even with the rings, I still can't really see the connection between the other two.'

Nodding once, Alain leaned forward. 'I don't know anything about the painter, but I can help you with the connection between Xavier and Wylène. Or at least with her boss, Chloé Walkure.'

Julie frowned. 'Go on.'

'I'll have to give you a little background info first. After I turned my little clothes shop into a high street empire, I got bored. What I told Jessica, that I was in construction, wasn't a complete lie, but it also wasn't the whole truth. It's more like I told you that night Thibault was shot. I look for struggling businesses to help them out. One of them was a construction company that I enjoyed working with enough to want to try to set one up myself. And the other thing I told you was true as well: I did get on the first bus and started walking around a random location to pick a venue for my new venture. I thought it had worked out better than I could have expected. The building was perfect, and its occupant even more so.'

Jessica's stomach tingled with a thousand butterflies. Alain might have lied to her, but he didn't know her then. Now that he did, he was just so utterly charming! She caught a look from Julie, who pressed her lips together but focussed on Alain when he continued.

'But then when I contacted the owner, he said the building was already in use. Since it clearly wasn't, I did some digging into the company that supposedly rented the building. The owner was a woman I'd already met at several functions: Wylène Chiche. It made sense, given the name.' He handed Julie the envelope.

Julie raised both eyebrows, making Jessica smile with glee. Alain was solving Xavier's murder so Jessica would go free. How had she ever doubted this man's hero status?

'When I told that police detective there was something fishy about the empty building that shouldn't be empty, he implied that Jessica was somehow involved as a scapegoat or even an accomplice to whatever was going on, since she was "part of the building", as he called it.' He cast Jessica an apologetic look.

'I should probably tell you that my father owns an insurance company for which I'd done some investigative leg work in the past. I asked Jessica to procure some paperwork for me while I snuck into Chloé's room to see if I could find anything pertaining to Jessica's building before the police would alert her to their interest in it. At the time, there was no evidence of anything illegal going on, but I installed a little listening device that has since picked up some very interesting material.'

Eager to contribute while Julie looked over the paperwork, Jessica chipped in, 'I thought it was strange that he would ask me to pick up those papers, but the woman at the gallery gave them to me without a second thought. Of course, she'd been at the reading of Xavier's will, so she knew the building now belonged to me. I called her after I heard Alain's story to ask her why she'd said it was one less thing to worry about, and she told me Xavier had left her with a whole bunch of shady deals she had had no knowledge of but that had somehow landed in her lap to handle.

'Of course, I already knew Xavier was a crook. But when I heard someone in the gallery ask why they'd given away her invoice, I was afraid I'd become a crook as well. Since I was still a suspect in Xavier's murder, I didn't want anything to do with all this building rental stuff. It wasn't until after I'd told Alain to leave that I found out the building was now mine and I'd have no choice but to deal with the rental stuff.'

Scratching the cat behind its ear, Julie stared at her coffee table. 'That takes care of the link between Wylène and Xavier, although I don't see why she would rent an empty building from Xavier. And it also doesn't explain why they were both killed on the same day as Roméo Paris. Unless...' Her eyes widened and she fumbled for her phone underneath the cat. Annoyed by her movement, it jumped off her lap and made for the cat flap in the double glass doors. Phone pressed to her ear, Julie impatiently tapped her leg. 'No answer. Of course. There's no reception at the commune.' She looked each of her guests in the eye. 'We need to go. Thibault could be in danger.'

Alain was already up. 'I'll drive.'

Trying to tame the horde of raging butterflies in her stomach, Jessica eyed the spring in his step before following. 'Isn't he amazing?' she whispered to Julie, but whether the photographer heard or not, there was no answer.

23

I'm on your side

The ancient little car swung from side to side with each turn of the road. I'd automatically veered towards my own car, but Jessica had gestured for me to get in the back of her 2CV, which Alain had already started.

'Come *on!*' Jessica had called, and for some reason, instead of driving my perfectly good Mini, I was now rapidly getting car sick in the back seat, a stiff bench in a car that was as old as *Conan the Barbarian*. Literally! Jessica was in the front, making goo-goo eyes at Alain, who had made it his mission to add as many turns as possible to the route to Jarnioux. At least twice another car honked at us for reckless driving. Exactly what Alain did, I had no idea, since I'd closed my eyes two minutes into the ride. Unfortunately, that left me with a queasy stomach that was already upset with worry over Beau. How I wished Léon was here! I don't know how I still managed to call Jacqueline and tell her to meet us at the artists' commune.

How had I not seen it before? It all fit together if it didn't fit together. With Jessica asking me for help in Xavier's murder and Beau needing my help with Wylène, I hadn't given enough attention to the death of Roméo Paris. Or maybe I should now call him Régis Piguemal. But the keys had done their job. Even though they were a glaringly obvious plant, this 'obvious fact' had still deceived me. Sorry, Sherlock, we can't all be you.

The car screeched to a stop, and I hurled myself out of the infernal machine, taking a deep breath as I stretched upright. That would have to do. We needed to find Beau. A big, provisional banner made from a painted sheet advertised a sale above the side entrance to Paris-Piguemal's garden and the studio in it, but apart from one or two obvious locals (a man with a paint-splattered apron and a woman covered in tufts of wool), the street lay abandoned. Tessa and Rosa could do with some advice on promotion.

Bypassing the house this time, we entered through the side entrance and found the door to the studio propped open. The first people I saw were the two girls. Rosa sat on the couch with her knees drawn up to her chest. Tessa leaned against the back of the couch, her arms and legs crossed in boredom, guarding a variety of large canvases and panels resting against the couch beside her.

My eyes searched for Beau but found Chloé instead. She stood facing the wall on the left, holding the edge of a painting she'd been looking at, now showing it to her left. Beau saw me before she did and didn't need more than the expression on my face to change his entire attitude from a lazy show of good-will to alert fury. Balling his fists, he turned back to Chloé.

'You?! You killed Wylène?'

Chloé's eyes widened. She lowered the canvas, finally noticing us by the door as she followed Beau's gaze. She huffed something between a nervous and a breezy laugh. 'What, your sugar aunt comes in, and you accuse me of murder? That's quite a leap, even for you.'

Excuse me? I paid him! Wait, that's not what I meant. I paid him to be my assistant!

But Beau focused on the insult to him, not to me. 'What's that supposed to mean, "even for me"? You've picked out the most random selection of works, one of which isn't even finished, and you've consistently been labelling them with the wrong style. You said you preferred Jessica's work from when she was in Provence, but Jess never sold anything in Marseille. You don't know anything about art, do you? You are supposed to be some kind of big-shot collector, but you needed Wylène to keep up the pretence.'

I was on the verge of applauding. Though he was off on the details, he'd found his own way to the heart of the matter.

Chloé snapped, 'I didn't need her. She needed me. More than she ever knew.'

'Is that why you killed her? To prove a point?'

Beau stepped forward, but Chloé recoiled, dropping the canvas, which hit the concrete with a crack. With one smooth movement, she drew a gun from her purse and aimed it at Beau. Behind me, I heard Jessica gasp, and my own knees wobbled. This was exactly what I'd come here to prevent! What could I do now?

'Huh. I thought you were just another yummy dummy. Guess I was wrong.' She sighed, glancing at us and towards the girls, who now both cowered behind the couch. 'All right, what's this going to be? A suicide pact? Do you all even know each other? Julie, go find some rope if you don't want me to shoot your pretty little toy boy.'

Me? She wanted me to do something? For *her*? But before I could display either willingness or unwillingness to do as she told me, my arms were pinned to my body and the cold metal of a blade rested against my skin. My blood turned to ice.

'I'm on your side, Chloé. Remember?' Alain's voice said in my ear.

Jessica screamed, and my blood unfroze with the heat of anger coursing through my body. Alain had turned against us? Or was he always against us? With the sound of my blood now rushing in my ears, I almost didn't register Chloé's words.

'Alain, what are you—'

As I lifted my elbow, Thibault lunged for the gun. Distracted by Alain's actions, Chloé saw him too late, and the gun flew out of her hand, skittering across the concrete floor. That's when my elbow landed firmly in Alain's solar plexus. The knife scraped my arm as Alain bent over, and I jumped away from him. Knowing nothing about fighting, I still put up my fists in a pitiful attempt to look imposing, until Beau's sarcastic tones filled the space.

'Well done, Julie, *ma minette*. You've successfully eliminated the guy trying to rescue you. You okay, *frérot*?'

I dropped my manicured fists, and turned to Beau, only taking my eyes off Alain when he started shaking with laughter. Beau was holding Chloé's arm twisted behind her back. Though her face was distorted with rage, she'd already given up the struggle.

Beau's gaze shifted from me to the door behind us. 'Ah, Jacqueline!' he said, chipper as can be. 'I believe this is yours?'

Once again, I turned round, only to see Jacqueline's grim smile as she walked past me toward Chloé and Beau, already pulling handcuffs from her belt. '*Merci bien*. I knew your snooping would come in handy one day.'

Was everyone in on this but me? 'You knew it was her?'

'I had my suspicions,' Jacqueline said while clicking the handcuffs in place. 'But I couldn't prove anything. I assumed that if I gave you just enough information, you might dig up something I couldn't access as a *flic*.'

'That's why I never became a cop.' Beau nodded. 'Too many rules.'

'Oh, *that's* it.' Jacqueline gave him a sideways grin, but my head was spinning.

'She could have killed us!' I felt like putting my claws in Jacqueline's face, but she only gave a perfect Gallic shrug.

'I did tell you to stay out of it.'

Marc Froment, Jacqueline's partner in crime fighting, huffed. He'd stayed well away from us, instead choosing to stand with the new owners of this barn still hidden on the couch.

Jessica, her hand glued to Alain's abs, seemed to be the only one less in the know than me. 'So... did she kill all of them?'

At that question, the girls on the couch poked their heads above the backrest.

'No.' I swallowed my rancour towards Jacqueline for the moment, so I could at least get credit for explaining what I'd found out. I nodded towards the girls. 'They killed Roméo, though I suspect it was Tessa who did the actual deed.'

Both girls gasped and shook their heads, but Beau said, 'I've had a look around, but all the Piguemals are gone.'

At this, Rosa's head snapped to Tessa, whose eyes bulged. 'I... I thought it would be best to hide them, so nobody would find out he made fakes.'

'Except they weren't fakes, were they?' I asked. 'Where did you put them?'

'Nowhere.' She slunk to the corner of the couch, away from Rosa's shocked eyes. 'I mean, I just hid them.'

'Chef Froment,' I addressed Jacqueline's colleague, 'I think you should have a look in Tessa's car.'

A tortured sob escaped Rosa's lips, while Tessa kept vigorously shaking her head. 'She did it,' Rosa cried. 'She convinced me my dad deserved to die for how he treated me. And all that time, you were just after his paintings?' The wail that followed was heart-rending, and both Jessica and I stepped forward to comfort her while Marc Froment handcuffed Tessa and read her her rights.

'But she came up with the idea,' Tessa spat. 'I didn't do this alone.'

'What was it you kept saying?' Rosa said through her tears. '"Prove it."' She turned to Marc Froment. 'I only said "I wish he was dead". She forced me to go along with it.'

'*Bien sûr,*' Marc said without much conviction. 'Follow me, please.'

Jacqueline guided Chloé to the door, too, but Chloé stopped to look at me down her nose. 'You didn't have any proof either, did you? I could have got away with it if that idiot hadn't attacked me.'

I waved the manilla envelope under her nose. 'That's where you're wrong. Beau didn't attack you, and we do have proof.'

'There's nothing in there that could prove I killed anyone.'

'Chiche-Kebab? You must have really hated her. Or did you pick that name because you hated yourself?'

Chloé narrowed her eyes.

'How did the police not find out it was Chloé you killed, Wylène? Because I'm sure they can find evidence for that now.'

Chloé, or rather Wylène, bared her teeth. 'Don't call me that! Wylène would always be second fiddle to Chloé. Even though she was happy for me to take all the credit and be in the limelight, I was still her puppet. Not that she would ever see it that way, oh no! Those morals were much too high. Sickening. She just wanted to be the brains in the background. I could take all the credit and all the respect. And believe me, I took it. Never had it before. But after five years of being Chloé, I knew exactly what to do. Why shouldn't it be me in charge?'

She took a deep breath, straightened, and looked me in the eye. 'Answer my question and I'll answer yours. How did you find out?'

'An old article in an architecture magazine mixed up your ages. I thought at first that at the time the article was written, you weren't very well known yet, so it must have been their mistake. But when I saw that you'd named your shell company Chiche-Kebab, it felt off. Spiteful. Who would want to make

Kebab of themselves, unless they didn't like who they were? But Wylène seemed nothing but happy, which both you and Beau confirmed. It made no sense for her to be resentful and menacing towards herself. If, however, you'd been posing as Chloé but were really Wylène—'

'*She* should have been Wylène!' the real Wylène burst out. 'She was everything I should have been. She was only seventeen when I met her, but her company was growing and she was starting to attract attention. She needed someone to legally sign along with her and she shunned the media attention that was starting to come with her rapid growth. She'd been able to handle deals with relative anonymity, but that was starting to prove more and more difficult. Neither of us had relatives or people who would remember us from before we switched roles, so from then on, the whole world would know us the other way round, even though officially, we still signed our given names to documents. I've always hated that name. Who in their right mind gives their child the initials W.C.? My life was in the toilet from the very start.'

She glared at me. 'You didn't have actual proof, did you? One old article and the name of a company. If you hadn't called me Wylène... I knew that name would be the death of me one day.'

Alain raised his hand and opened his mouth. Maybe his bug had actually caught something, but Wylène cut him off. 'But you were right too. You would have been able to find evidence for that theory. Plenty of it. We never legally changed anything, so that was the main weakness in my plan to get rid of her. But if people can name their price, all you have to do is find the little person who does the filing. They're usually the cheapest too. It took me a while to locate the right person in the right place, but I finally had it all worked out.'

'Until Xavier found out.'

She gave me an open-mouthed frown. 'How do you know these things?'

I shrugged. That one was actually a lucky guess. It could just as easily have had to do with the fake company.

'Yes, he talked Chloé into a contract where he would supply us with more art. We signed the papers there and then, but unlike most people, he noticed we signed our own names and realised he'd been dealing with what he called 'the underling'. And if that was the case, that I'd been stealing from the company and laundering it through him and his art. Chloé never even realised that the art we bought from him was paid for with money from a different account.'

'And that's why you thought you could run the company by yourself,' Beau said, probably remembering her state when we went to visit this morning. 'But as it turned out, you really were just an underling.'

I winced at Beau's mean words, understandable as they were. But before Wylène could react, Jessica joined in.

'And Xavier wanted money to keep quiet, didn't he? Typical.'

W.C. – I thought that moniker fitted – nodded. 'He would have ruined my careful set-up. So I sneaked out of the floatation tank, drove to his office, and bashed him over the head with the first thing I could find.'

I almost punched the air in victory. I knew that rash wasn't from stress! She hadn't taken the time to rinse off properly and the Epsom salts from the water in the tank had wreaked havoc on her scalp. 'But if you already had an alibi, why don your gloves and Xavier's rings to wave at whoever saw you?'

'Double precaution. After ten, I had an appointment with a mayor who'd swear I was with her and several others. Just in case there was some sort of alarm on those tanks or someone had seen me leave. I couldn't be sure if someone would recognise those rings, of course, but it was all I could come up with on such short notice. Lo and behold, I only helped the prime suspect in his murder case make herself look more unreliable. I couldn't have planned it better if I tried.'

'Is that why you left the rings here too? As a precaution?' Jacqueline asked.

W.C. looked over her shoulder. 'I would call that more of a misdirection, wouldn't you? I'd left the keys in the car with the door open when I parked it in Villefranche, counting on some unscrupulous person to take care of it for me. I don't know why I didn't just leave the rings in the car... Maybe they felt too personal. Or maybe I had a subconscious idea of using them the way that I did. I really can't remember.'

'Kind of an obvious plant, though.'

'Perhaps, but I needed to get rid of them, so when I overheard Julie talk about them at the gallery, I knew where to leave them with no trace back to me.'

'Like the *grattons*?' I asked, kicking myself for discussing the case in a public place and hoping Jacqueline wouldn't pick up on that. 'How come the police didn't find them when they searched your room?'

She laughed. 'That was even easier! Because they weren't really looking. They assumed Wyl— Chloé would have hidden her stash in her own room and only searched mine to be thorough. Ha! I'd already flushed the poisoned *grattons* and flung the bag out of the window to let the wind do the rest.'

'But why tell everyone you thought her death was no accident? Nobody would have doubted your innocence.' Except maybe Jacqueline, but she would have had to obey her boss.

W.C. shrugged. 'Underline my grief. Take away any doubt I was involved should anyone start digging. I didn't think you would actually start poking your nose in.'

'Right. I'll let you write all of that down and sign it at the station.' Jacqueline had indulged me long enough. She probably felt guilty about using me as bait, but this little exchange wasn't nearly enough payment for what she'd done.

She'd already passed me when she turned round again. 'Good work. On all accounts. I still thought the painter and the art dealer were connected. How did you figure that one out?'

'We saw Rosa crying in Tessa's arms on the day of the murders. When I found out she was Roméo's daughter, I thought she must have been crying over his death, but then I realised it was before he'd been killed. On its own, that didn't prove anything, but if it meant Roméo's death was the one not connected to the others, everything else fit.'

Jacqueline nodded. Then she led Wylène out the door and followed without another word.

Thibault dramatically clutched his heart. 'A compliment! From Jacqueline! Was it real? Did I dream it?'

Jessica and Alain laughed at his clowning around. I chuckled along but didn't feel all that much relief. For years, people had easily believed W.C. was the successful one, simply because she was older. Not a doubt in anyone's mind that the younger must be the assistant. Part of me wanted to be happy that for once, it had not been the young, pretty one to be the face of the company. But for the older, less pretty face, that had not been enough. Jealousy was an awful thing.

I smiled at Jessica. 'Tell me, real artist, how did you know so quickly that the Jessica Rose statue in the Centre was fake? You said yourself you can't tell them apart.'

She raised an eyebrow with her smile at the way I addressed her but let it go. 'That's why I asked you for the serial number. Every time I finish one of my blobs, I put the mileage of my car on the bottom. Xavier made up numbers that wouldn't even be close.'

Alain put his arms around her from behind, and my smile soured as I reached to stroke the wound on my arm. 'Do you think I'll ever be as important to you as that car?' he asked with his lips against her cheek.

'You can try.' She giggled. She really had the worst taste in men.

Surveying the barn filled with paintings, I wondered what would happen to them now. Beau stood next to me and rested his arm on my shoulder. 'What a waste,' he said, seeming to guess my thoughts. 'Come on, let's go. You did what you could.'

Reluctantly, I followed the others out of the barn and closed the door behind me. 'Jessica? Which one is Anaëlle's house?'

'Oh! Good one.' She faced left, but then turned to me. 'Don't worry, I'll make sure she knows what happens so she can take care of Rosa and the art. You've done enough.' She stepped closer and hugged me. 'Thank you so much for clearing my name. If it weren't for you, that other policeman would still consider me a murderess.' She let go and started towards Anaëlle's before she stopped again. 'Give me ten minutes and I'll take you home.'

Oh no. Not the dreaded waggle wagon.

'I'll do that.' Beau jingled a bunch of keys before my eyes. 'I still have the killer's car keys.'

Despite that car's connections, I sighed with relief. 'Thank the Lady. Oh, and I am not your kitten.'

24

Yummy dummy

'To me she'll always be Wylène.'

Beau hung diagonally on my couch, one leg on the ground, the other pulled up on the seat, a beer dangling from his fingers. Though he'd tried to lift the mood after Jacqueline had taken W.C. away, his own mood had gone dark as soon as we were in the car. He was happy the killer was behind bars, of course, but that didn't stop him resenting her. He probably always would.

'That's who she chose to be, so I don't think she'd mind.' We'd been sitting here for a while, me with my book – but dreaming about Léon – and him with a sketchbook beside him, though he hadn't touched it yet.

He took another sip, then suddenly got up. 'I think we should open our Easter eggs.'

I looked up from my book and raised my eyebrows. Two large chocolate eggs, one wrapped in blue, one wrapped in pink, had been sitting on my dresser for the last week, when I bought them as a joke. They weren't supposed to be touched for another week, but if Beau needed something fun, he was welcome to them.

'Which one do you want?' he asked.

The pink one. 'The blue one.'

He handed me the pink. 'If you want pink, just say so.'

Opening the pink foil, I gave him a secret glare. He was getting to know me far too well.

Mouth full of chocolate, he sat back down on the couch, but not in the lethargic position he'd had before. 'Juju... You think I'm a yummy dummy?'

I almost spat out my chocolate. 'Of course not! Why would you say such a thing? You can't give credit to what a person says when you're about to ship her off to jail. And also, she said you were *not* a yummy dummy.'

'But you said you wouldn't want to spoil my reputation.'

I winced. 'I was angry. And hurt.' I took a breath. 'And jealous.'

A small smile played around the corner of his mouth. 'You have no reason to be jealous. Of anyone.'

Did my heart jump a little bit at those words? Not just a little. I was about to get up and hug him when he cast down his gaze, fiddling with a piece of blue foil.

'What *is* my reputation?'

My first instinct was to go 'How should I know?', but I wouldn't get away with that. 'I suppose... some people... think you're a bit of a *chacal*, a flirt.'

He huffed a humourless laugh, keeping his eyes trained on the piece of foil.

'But you don't...' How should I put this? 'Get paid for it, right?'

Then he looked up. 'No! Is that what people say?'

I gave an apologetic shrug. 'Not anyone who really knows you, of course.'

He folded the foil in half twice before he spoke, and I had to lean forward to hear what he said.

'It's... *I'm*... just a bit of fun.'

I couldn't help it. I burst out laughing. He frowned at me, but I shook my head. 'Now you're just being ridiculous. Look at how much you've learned since you came here. You can do anything you want!'

'The world is your oyster. Make sure you have a knife.' He smirked at the bandage I'd put on my arm even though the scratch was barely visible any more, but I refused to let him deter me.

'Look at how much you've helped me, and I don't just mean at work. And that's just me! You know some of the people in the village better than I do, because in six months, you've become a part of this community. Nobody in their right mind would think of you as "just a bit of fun".'

My stomach contracted as I realised that was what had been keeping him from posing for me. That was also why he hadn't been out of sorts when Yolande had bossed him around. He thought he was 'just a bit of fun', but her fun had been respectful. I thought he'd dismissed my art as frivolous, but my art was fine. It just wasn't for him, as to him it put the emphasis on being, rather than having, fun. Now that I'd taken care of my own insecurities, I could try to eradicate his. 'Here, give me that sketchbook.'

It was a long shot, because he usually guarded his sketchbooks like a mother hen her chicks, but I knew from stolen glances that what was in there was quality art.

He narrowed his eyes at me but handed over the book, which I opened at random in the middle. 'Look at this. These yogis checking each other out are brilliant! And this dad building a tiny den out of twigs with his son. Beautiful.' I turned the page. 'Wow. This portrait of Céline is gorgeous.' I looked again, only half noticing that he'd stopped making derogatory noises. I tilted my head and flipped back a few pages. The girl he was always drawing... I flipped back more. How had I not seen this before? The vaguely familiar, generic girl had been Céline from the start.

I looked up. Beau's jaw muscles were working overtime, and not on the chocolate. He stared at the book on my lap to avoid looking at me. Céline had a boyfriend. For just about as long as he'd been sulking.

'So, do you hate him very much?'

He pressed his lips together, then gave a reluctant smile. 'Unfortunately, he's a great guy. *Sympa*, you know? He just wants us to be friends.'

'Hm. I hate to say it, but... maybe it's time to start drawing another girl.'

Slowly nodding, he sighed. 'I know. But it's not that easy. You know how you talk to Léon every day? Céline and I talk every day, face to face, but it still feels like there's an ocean between us. Especially now, with Chito there all the time. Oh, that reminds me.'

He fished his phone out of his pocket, scrolled for a bit, and handed it to me. 'I'm sorry I wasn't at your party, Juju. Truly. For what it's worth, my mum's got your back. When I was there, I heard her threaten my dad with divorce if he let Franck hurt you. Here, Céline sent me this after the party.'

I played the video he showed me. I cringed when I saw myself break down and cry, but then the camera panned slightly, focussing on my brother David. He shifted uncomfortably at my display of emotion but then saw Maëline next to him brush away a tear, conquered his own stuffiness, and pulled her close.

'Aww! He finally made it.' I beamed at Beau, trying my best to embrace his change of subject. 'We should bring him some champagne or something. Actually, I prefer Crémant de Bourgogne. Do we have any left? Or did we drink the last one to celebrate your Piguemal being real after all?'

'You realise that was only this morning, right?'

I blinked at him, speechless.

'What I don't understand,' he continued, 'is why they wanted to sell the paintings now. Wouldn't they have been worth ten times as much when the world found out Piguemal had continued painting?'

'Perhaps.' I cooed at Henri, who'd strutted in through the cat flap and now jumped on my lap. 'I suspect they wanted to cash in as much as they could in case anyone found out they killed him and they'd have to run. But – and you're not going to like this – with all those Piguemals flooding the market, the price of them might well take a tumble instead.'

'*Ah, oui*, I hadn't thought of that. But it doesn't affect me. I won't sell it anyway. It's a gorgeous piece of art that will always remind me of you and this case. And, of course, of how you nearly died.'

He stroked his own arm at the place where I'd bandaged mine. But I had the last laugh. My well-aimed cushion hit him straight in his pretty face.

Other books by Christa Bakker

Acknowledgements

My deepest thanks, as always, go to Kristen Tate at The Blue Garret, who helps me take my stories out into the world with confidence and pride, knowing they're the best they could be.

Carole Marples deserves no less gratitude, as she deals with most of my sighing and moaning during the process of getting the words onto the page. I don't know if I could do it without her.

Thank you as well to my mother, who is always one of the first to read and rave about a new story. *Jij bent mijn heldin.*

And, last but not least, my husband and children always get my love and gratitude for keeping me in cuddles. Never ever stop!

Editing by Kristen Tate at The Blue Garret

Book cover by Christa and Erik Bakker

1st edition 2024

ISBN: 978-1-916998-05-6

Visit the author's website at: www.christabakker.com

www.ingramcontent.com/pod-product-compliance
Lightning Source LLC
Chambersburg PA
CBHW061520210726
48287CB00006B/1756